Praise for *The Team*

"Dave Salkin's *The Team* series describes real-world action and suspense and puts you in the middle of spec-ops action. While reading them, I could feel the recoil in my shoulder pocket, smell the powder burning and feel like I was reliving the times that I embraced the suck!"

- Colonel William L Peace, Sr., US Army Support Group Commander, Desert Storm and OIF Veteran

D1310175

A POST HILL PRESS BOOK
ISBN: 978-1-68261-175-3
ISBN (eBook): 978-1-61868-857-6

The Team:
Book One
© 2016 by David M. Salkin
All Rights Reserved

Cover Design by David Walker

Post Hill Press
posthillpress.com

Published in the United States of America

THE TEAM

DAVID M. SALKIN

Also by David M. Salkin

Hard Carbon
Deep Black Sea
Dark Tide Rising

The Team Series Continues
Into the Jungle
African Dragon
Shadow of Death
The MOP

The TEAM

Coach: Chris Mackey, CIA

US Navy Seals:
Chris Cascaes, Chief Petty Officer, SEAL team leader
Al "Moose" Carlogio
Vinny "Ripper" Colgan
Ray Jensen
Pete McCoy
Jon Cohen
Ryan O'Conner

Marine Recondos:
Eric Hodges
Earl Jones
Raul Santos

Army Rangers:
Lance Woods
Jake Koches

CIA:
Ernesto "Ernie P." Perez
Joe "Smitty" Smith
Cory Stewart

"An appeaser is one who feeds a crocodile, hoping it will eat him last."

Winston Churchill

This book is dedicated to

Master Sergeant Gary Gordon
and
Sergeant First Class Randy Shughart.
Both recipients of the Medal of Honor
Killed in Action,
Battle of Mogadishu, Somalia
October 1993.

And Corporal Patrick Daniel "Pat" Tillman—Army
Ranger, NFL Star, and American Patriot—who left a
successful NFL career to serve his country and made the
ultimate sacrifice on April 22, 2004 in Afghanistan.
The Heart of a Lion.

And Corporals Jonathan Yale and Lance Corporal Jordan
Haerter, USMC, who stood their ground in the face of certain
death and saved fifty of their brothers on April 22, 2008 near
Ramadi. Their Navy Crosses seem so small compared to their
actions. Their heroism is briefly memorialized in this book as
a tribute to these courageous young Marines.

And finally, to my friend George Etlinger,
gone before his time.

Thanks for all the laughs, George. You are missed.

ACKNOWLEDGEMENTS

This book, although a work of fiction, is based on a real military operation that took place in the late 1960s in Southeast Asia. I would like to thank Al C. (whose last name I will not reveal) for the information he shared with me as a US Navy frogman fighting in Vietnam. Al, known as Moose to his friends, was a "UDT" Underwater Demolition Team frogman. This group of specialized operators would later evolve into what we know today as Navy SEALs.

Al and his team were mostly Warrant Officers, and they were put together on a fictitious Navy All-Star Baseball team. It was their job to show baseball to the people of Southeast Asia as an exhibition team—playing against other service branches or locals who could put together a scratch team on short notice. The fifteen of them toured South Vietnam, Cambodia, and Laos playing baseball. There were fifteen men on their roster. There were never more than eleven in the dugout. Where were the other four? They were out "working"—and it wasn't playing baseball.

When this idea was first showed to a publisher, they said it was a great story, but it wasn't believable. Al laughed when I told him that. He was happy in a way, and said, "It was a good cover story after all, wasn't it?" Yes it was, Al. Good enough that it deserves to be told…

For Al and his team, who risked life and limb for their country, thank you for your service and for sharing your story with me.

CHAPTER 1

January 2012, Hawaii

While on a two-week liberty in Hawaii, Chris Mackey had been relaxing and doing some beer drinking on the beach with Chris Cascaes and a few of his SEALs. They had all become pretty tight after working together on a counter-terrorism operation, code named "Crescent Fire." After a couple of days of sleeping like hibernating bears, the exhausted men recovered and got bored. The next few days turned into a combination drink-fest/ tail-chasing marathon, which eventually slowed down and led to some beach volleyball and finally to a few baseball games.

The baseball games ended up becoming real games— competitive natured guys who were in primo physical shape and didn't like losing, taking on other competitive natured guys who were in primo physical shape and also didn't like losing. The beach where they were staying was a popular spot with enlisted men from every branch of the service, as well as tourists, and there was no shortage of testosterone-pumped young guys wanting to be the next Babe Ruth. The game became a daily ritual, always played at eleven in the morning, which allowed at least five hours of sleep after an entire evening of the afore-mentioned drinking and tail chasing.

Cascaes, Mackey, and the bunch of Navy SEALs added a few Marine Recondos, a couple of Army Rangers, and three CIA operatives, who had been imbedded with the Army

Rangers in Afghanistan that Mackey knew, to their team, and they proceeded to take on all-comers each day.

By the fourth day in a row of grueling baseball games, Mackey volunteered to be official coach, as he was completely exhausted. Cascaes, a SEAL through and through, would not allow himself to verbalize his physical pain, nor show his crew that he was indeed getting older. He did, however, make second base his official position on the team, where he hoped he wouldn't have to run or throw too far.

It was on the sixth day, while drinking beer and watching the huge Ensign they called Moose strike out his sixth batter in three innings, that Mackey's light bulb went off.

He nudged Cascaes and commented as a Marine struck out and threw his bat. "Ya know, these guys are *really* good."

The two men were sitting back in low beach chairs, feet buried in the sand, surrounded by a copious amount of squashed empty beer cans. The sun was getting low on the horizon, and the beer can collection had started when it was high overhead.

Cascaes finished his cold can and burped. "Yeah, well, *we* used to be twenty-one, too."

"No, no," Mackey said smiling, "I mean these guys are *really* good. You know much about special operations in Vietnam?"

"What the hell does that have to do with baseball?" asked Cascaes.

"Do you?" he asked again.

"No, Mack. I am practically young enough to be your son—I wasn't old enough for 'Nam," he said sarcastically.

"Yeah, well, *I* was there. Remember hearing about the Phoenix Project?"

"Yeah—assassinations and Black Ops," said Cascaes.

"I wasn't involved in that stuff. I was flying recon planes over the jungle and getting holes in my plane while I tried to take pictures. But I had a few friends from 'Nam that I used to shoot the shit with back in the day. We were all in Intelligence so we used to talk a little, you know? Not about the *most* secret shit but about general stuff we still weren't supposed to talk about."

"So?" asked Cascaes, now fully interested.

"Strike three!" yelled somebody in the background.

"Well, one of my buddies in the Navy—he was UDT—underwater demolition team. Before the SEALs..."

"Yeah, I know what UDT is, Mack."

"Well, you being so *young* and all, I wasn't sure you'd know," he said sarcastically. "Anyway, my buddy, he told me a story about a baseball team. I think I have an idea..."

◈

It took four strong men to move the large wooden crate from the truck to the boat. They were working under the cover of night in a small commercial marina that had no activity at three in the morning. The boat was a rust-bucket that had been used for cargo since the Second World War, but was inconspicuous enough to be perfect for smuggling. Once the crate was aboard, it was tarped and covered with other cargo, and the small boat began its voyage from Lebanon to Egypt.

CHAPTER 2

January 2012, Hawaii

It was the bottom of the ninth and getting hot as hell—over ninety-five degrees. If the SEALs hadn't just come home from a year operating in Iraq and Afghanistan, they might have noticed. Instead, they laughed and joked as they played in the humid Hawaiian sun, still running at full speed while the sweat ran down into their sneakers. The locals they were playing, who were also used to the heat, were not smiling or joking because the score was eleven to nothing. They shouldn't have been too ashamed—the SEALs and Marine Recondos had beaten an Air Force team the day before by fifteen runs.

After Al "Moose" Carlogio struck out the last batter to end the game, his catcher jogged up to the mound to high-five him. Vinny "Ripper" Colgan, the catcher, had been Moose's dive-buddy for so long they didn't even have to use signals half the time. It was only fitting that they were a pitcher-catcher duo, since they'd been buddies in every operation in and out of the water for the past seven years.

"Jesus, man. You keep this up and I'm gonna have to get a new catcher's mitt. I bet your fastball was hitting ninety-five today. My hand *hurts*," he said with a broad smile. Something about the gap between his two front teeth just made him look more like a catcher.

Vinny was as broad as Moose and two inches taller at six-four. They were the biggest guys on the SEAL team, the rest

4

being between five-ten and six-foot with medium builds. Everyone always assumed SEALs were huge, but in fact most were average-sized guys who were just too stubborn to ever quit anything.

Moose smiled. "Yeah, I was *on* today. I think I throw better when it's hot like this. I'm about ready to swim—you in?"

"After a cold one," said Ripper with a grin as he headed to the bench.

The rest of the team jogged in and they converged on the cooler under the bench. A couple of the locals came over and shared a beer or joke, but they left pretty quickly, sensing that they were definitely outsiders. Even though the team was comprised of Navy, Marines, CIA, and Army, they had bonded pretty quickly and dropped the usual inter-service ribbing. They had started playing very well as a team and had really enjoyed destroying the teams they played against every day.

As soon as they threw back a beer, Moose announced it was "time to get wet"—a phrase they had all learned to hate in BUDs[1] training but now considered just a part of everyday life. The SEALs, including their commanding officer, Chris Cascaes, didn't wait for a second call. They all started running to the beach a few hundred yards away, stripping as they went. A trail of shirts, sneakers, socks, baseball gloves, batting gloves, and baseball hats stretched from the bench to the beach. The Army Rangers and CIA operatives just laughed and shook their heads at the SEALs as they splashed their way into the waves.

As they did every day after the game, the SEALs swam two miles, including two twenty-five yard underwater swims. All this *after* playing baseball in the sun for hours and getting drunk the night before. Moose and Ripper, two of the more senior team members, made sure the group stayed in top shape

---

[1] Basic Underwater Demolition/SEAL school. This is the beginning of the long, seemingly impossible route to becoming a US Navy SEAL.

at all times. On missions, there was a great sense of confidence that came from knowing you could swim or run forever and never get tired. And, as life usually goes, you never knew when a mission was going to come your way—hence every day was training day. The SEALs typically sang out in unison, "the only easy day was yesterday," their unofficial motto.

While the SEALs swam, Jake Koches and Lance Wood, the two Army Rangers, finished another couple of beers and recapped exploits from the night before. Their laughter attracted the three Marines and three CIA operatives, who sat down next to them and listened with great amusement to how two Rangers ended up with three nurses in one hotel room. The story was just getting explicitly interesting when Chris Mackey plopped into the sand next to them and interrupted their little story.

"You guys play some serious ball," said Mackey.

"My man Hodges took the cover off that sumbitch today!" said Earl Jones, one of the Marines, about one of his fellow Jarheads. His smile and laugh were contagious.

Eric Hodges, a wiry little redhead from Oklahoma, flashed a toothy grin. "Yeah, baby. I got *all* of that one today." He exchanged a fancy handshake with Earl Jones.

"Any of you guys play in college?" asked Mackey.

Jones laughed loudly. "*College*? If I went to college already, I wouldn't be humpin' around Afghanistan and Iraq!" He laughed and gave Hodges another handshake.

"What about you guys?" asked Mackey, looking at the rest of them. They mostly exchanged glances, not wanting to be the "nerd who went to college" after Jones' comment.

"I played at Rutgers," said Jake Koches after another second went by. He was ROTC in college and was a second lieutenant in the Rangers.

"Southern Cal for two years," said Lance. "Then I dropped out. The surfin' was just *too* good." That brought a few more chuckles.

Ernesto Perez, a CIA operative who had been working embedded with the Rangers for two years in Afghanistan, 'fessed up to playing in Puerto Rico his entire life, but he never made it to college. "Ernie P." as they called him, alternated pitching with Moose. When he wasn't pitching, he played outfield and could put the ball on home plate from anywhere inside the stadium. Joe Smith, "Smitty", CIA, and Cory Stewart, also CIA, both played growing up, but nothing serious. Even so, they were both great infielders, and Smitty could hit the ball a mile. Perez, Smith, and Stewart—for the purposes of hangin' with the fellas—were all government contractors, but the entire team knew exactly whom they worked for. Perez had actually worked with Lance and Jake in Afghanistan, and they assumed his buddies were also CIA.

They talked baseball for a while, and finally Chris Mackey floated out an idea to the little group. "How would you guys like to stay together for a while playing some baseball and doing some traveling? You'd be with our Navy buddies out there, assuming they don't get eaten by sharks."

"Man, I think it's the *sharks* that gotta worry," said Jones. "Them muthafuckers is part *fish*, man. They swim more in a day then I done in my whole *life*."

Everyone laughed.

"Ain't no beach on 150th Street," he added.

"Yeah, you might be right about the sharks," said Mackey, scanning the ocean horizon for the SEALs, who had swum out almost a mile.

"What do you mean about staying and playing baseball?" Hodges asked Mackey.

"Not staying *here*. And not partying every day either. I'm talking about *working*. Using a baseball team as a cover and traveling around as an All-Star team of sorts. We'd use the cover to get in and out of countries where you'd be working."

The CIA agents looked at each other and smiled. Mackey caught the glances. "What do you think?" he asked them.

"No comment," said Smitty.

"Why not?" asked Mackey.

"Let's just say it wouldn't be the most unusual thing I ever heard of. If you end up putting it together, I'll play ball," he said with a grin.

Ernie P. and Cory looked at each other. Ernie spoke up. "Well shit, man. If he's gonna play, I'll play. You're gonna need another pitcher."

Hodges, with his slow Oklahoma drawl, looked around at the others and then at Mackey. "So let me get this right. Y'all gonna make a fake baseball team and do secret agent shit with it?"

Jones laughed at him, then mimicked his voice as best he could with his New York accent, "*Y'all gonna do secret agent shit?*" He laughed and high-fived Raul Santos, the other Marine.

Raul, who was usually quiet, whispered, "We're gonna be secret agents and kill bad guys."

The crowd laughed and shook their heads at Raul, who rarely cracked a smile but was occasionally hilarious.

Mackey was smiling but serious. "Yeah, that's basically the idea. I'm thinking that we could put together a baseball demonstration team. Travel around spreading good will and showing the world American Baseball. And then occasionally steal state secrets or whack a bad guy." He smiled.

They all agreed that they would do it if it ever came to fruition. They were just finishing up their conversation when the SEALs came jogging up the beach in a column of twos singing the theme from Gilligan's Island. They had just swum a few miles, after playing baseball in killer heat for almost two and half hours, and now they were running in the sand singing like idiots. Mackey grinned. Hell—they could make a baseball team, a football team, a skydiving team—just about *anything* out of those guys.

Chris Mackey would later speak to Chris Cascaes about his idea, and Cascaes would be equally excited, immediately volunteering his SEAL team should the baseball team ever be assembled.

⊕

The boat had been sailing around the waters off of Egypt for hours, waiting for a time that was too late for working men and too early for fishermen. At a little before four in the morning, the boat chugged into a tiny marina near Alexandria that was typically used by commercial fishermen. It was dark, and the boat slipped into an open berth where it was met by four men who helped unload the heavy crate and move it to their truck.

A bag of cash was exchanged and the truck drove quickly to the small airstrip not far from the dock. A small birdcage sat on top of the crate that had been secured to the walls and floor of the cargo plane. Should the bird die, the crew knew they would only have seconds to open the cargo ramp to air out the plane and make an emergency landing. The two men in the back of the plane stared at the bird for the entire trip from Alexandria to Saudi Arabia.

CHAPTER 3

Al Qaisumah, Saudi Desert

Abu Mohamed sat silently in the box truck watching the air strip in the moonless night. It had been a long three weeks—the planning, the payoffs, and every mode of transportation known to man. It had been very stressful, even for a seasoned arms dealer like himself.

"There," whispered the driver, Kalif. He pointed to the lights of a plane getting closer. An ancient cargo plane slowed and descended. The tires chirped twice as it touched down and cruised to a stop at the end of the long runway. The twin props cut off with a few coughs and a long dying whine.

"Go," said Abu quietly.

Kalif put the truck in gear and drove out to the tarmac behind the plane. The cargo door lowered slowly, opening the belly of the plane under the tail. Low lights inside revealed four men in coveralls who were releasing cables and hooks from a large wooden crate, which they then rolled carefully down the ramp.

Kalif drove in a half circle then slowly backed the truck up towards the cargo ramp until one of the men patted the rear of the vehicle a few times to signal "stop." Abu's two men in the cab silently hopped down and jogged to the rear of the truck where they lowered the tailgate. The six men then pushed the box to the edge, hoisted the lift until it was level with the back of the truck, and pushed it inside. Once centered in the truck, cables and heavy straps were attached to the crate to secure it. After a few test tugs, the men hopped down and closed the tailgate.

Kalif jogged up the ramp of the plane, handed the pilot a heavy duffle bag full of cash, and jogged back to the truck. Once inside, he pulled away quickly with the four of them sitting in complete silence. By the time they were out of the tiny airport, the cargo plane was taxiing down the runway on its way back to Egypt.

Abu watched the plane bank left and smiled. The Sarin had been stolen and smuggled from Syria to Lebanon by truck. In Lebanon, it was transferred to a boat which sailed to Egypt near Alexandria, where it was loaded aboard the ancient cargo plane and flown to Al Qaisumah in the Saudi Arabian desert, about three hundred kilometers from the Kuwait border. There had been payoffs every step of the way. It would now make its way along the extensive sun-baked highway known as "Eighty-Five" until it turned into "Seventy-Five" and got them close to the Qatar border at Al Hofuf. Once Abu made it to Al Hofuf, his mission would be over, and he could enjoy the life of a rich prince.

CHAPTER 4

January 2012, Hawaii

Chris Mackey and Chris Cascaes had used a secure phone in their gear to call Dexter "Dex" Murphy, the Middle East Assistant Desk Chief back in Langley. Dex had run the Crescent Fire operation with them the previous December and was the number-two man for Middle East Intelligence in the CIA after Darren Davis, the Desk Chief.

At forty-nine, Dex was considered young to be the number two man in the busiest section of the CIA, but he had proven himself to be a highly intelligent and creative chief. His reddish-brown hair was getting salty from way too many hours at his job—a schedule that his wife tolerated because she knew his job was designed to keep their children safe from Middle Eastern terrorists. Dex had a small build, and too many hours at a desk was starting to make him soft in the middle, which his wife did *not* tolerate. As a result, it wasn't uncommon for Dex to be found doing push-ups or sit-ups in his office, while wearing a shirt and tie. Dex had an understanding with his two secretaries— any work week that extended beyond seventy hours triggered a bouquet of flowers being sent to his wife. He credited them and the florist with saving his marriage. A few eighty hour weeks resulted in jewelry, also picked out by his secretaries.

It took a few phone calls back and forth to coordinate their conversation, but finally Mackey got Dex on the phone, with Cascaes sitting next to him in Mackey's hotel room.

"Hey, Mack, good to hear your voice," said Dex. "Enjoying your R and R on the beach, I trust?"

"You know it, baby. But you know how easily I get bored. I'm here with Chris Cascaes. We've hatched an idea that I want to run by you."

"You're supposed to be on vacation—what are you guys up to now?" asked Dex with a laugh. Dex was very well acquainted with Cascaes from prior missions involving his SEAL Team.

"Can you talk now?" asked Mackey. "I mean, we're on a secure phone. Are you alone right now?"

"Yeah, go ahead. I'm secure here. Now you've got my interest piqued," said Dex.

"Well, it's just an idea, really. I can't even take credit for it—it's not new. Back in Vietnam, I knew a guy that played on a baseball team that wasn't a baseball team. They used to tour around Southeast Asia as a baseball exhibition team playing local teams and teaching baseball. They'd roster like fifteen guys but never had more than eleven or twelve in the dugout. The other guys would be *working*, know what I mean?"

Dex was smiling on his end of the phone, thinking about a soccer team that currently had two agents on it in Mexico. He only knew about it because they had once played in the United Arab Emirate and he was given a heads-up prior to a hit on a "most wanted" from his section.

"Yeah, I follow you. What are you concocting now?"

"Well, we've been playing baseball for over a week, and the guys on our little team are serious athletes—I mean *really* good. I think some of these guys could make it professionally, no kidding. Anyway, they're SEALs, Recondos, Rangers, and a trio from our neck of the woods. The SEALs are Cascaes' crew, and they are *hardcore*. Anyway, I'd like you to run background on all these guys and see what you think. Personally, I think these guys could do just about anything. What if they were a Navy All-Star team or something and traveled around playing teams from other countries? It would be a great way to get in and out of places."

"Send me an email with your roster—names and social security numbers, branch of service, etcetera, and we'll look into it. Like you said, what you are proposing has been done before, so we have to consider how effective it could be, but I'll run it past Darren and see what he says. In the meantime, try and get some rest and stay out of trouble. I'll talk to you later, after I get your email."

"Okay, see ya later, Dex." Mackey hung up and repeated the message to Cascaes.

"Well, he didn't say no," said Cascaes.

Six days later, a new file was opened in Dexter Murphy's office, simply referred to as "The Team."

CHAPTER 5

Chris Mackey, the coach of the baseball team, was briefing his men in the back of a chartered commercial jet as they flew from Germany to Saudi Arabia. He and his players were the only passengers besides the flight crew in the cockpit. There were no flight attendants, and the flight crew knew they were not to interrupt the meeting in the back of the aircraft. Instead of eating peanuts and watching a movie, the passengers watched a slide show of Middle Eastern maps and people.

Coach Mackey, a CIA operative for over twenty years, was the team leader of this Navy All-Star Exhibition Team. His fifteen men were all great athletes and excellent baseball players—good enough that they could compete with almost any minor league team around. The truth was, it really didn't matter if they lost one hundred to nothing, and they weren't touring all over the world because they needed to win on the baseball diamond.

Mackey stood before the fifteen players seated in front of him and began his presentation. The first slide came up showing Eskan Village, the home to a few thousand US personnel stationed in Saudi.

"This is Eskan Village, outside Riyadh. Any of you been there before?" asked Mackey.

The Army Rangers, Marine Recondos, and one of the CIA operatives raised their hands. When Mackey made eye contact

15

with the CIA agent, an agent by the name of Cory Stewart, Cory shrugged and smiled and added, "*Allegedly.*"

"Well, for those of you who haven't been there, Eskan is where most Air Force personnel live who work in Riyadh. The place is clean and well maintained, except for the occasional pile of camel shit. It was originally built by the Saudi government for the Bedouins, but they preferred their tents and camels, and the place was abandoned until we started using it." He changed slides to a road map of northern Saudi Arabia, showing roads from Riyadh through the Northern Border leading to Iraq. "These are the main roads from the capital to Iraq. It appears that *zaqat* money—that's money the locals give to charity—is ending up in Iraq funding the insurgency. I'm happy to say that our job isn't very complicated. We're merely pulling an armed robbery." He smiled and paused.

Earl Jones, a Marine Recondo from Harlem, couldn't help speaking up. "Yo, man, you better let *me* have a whack at *this* job. I wasn't *always* a poster boy for the United States Marine Corps." He laughed loudly and gave Raul Santos, another Marine, a long 150th Street handshake.

Mackey smiled. "As a matter of fact, Jones, you *are* on this job—now shut up." Mackey used a laser pointer to illuminate one of the small lines on the screen. "This road here is a little off the beaten track. Our Intelligence in Saudi tells us that money and weapons have been moved along this route into Iraq. Apparently, there is a major bankroll headed north in a couple of days."

Mackey changed slides again, this time to a picture of a fruit truck. "This little piece of crap truck is our target, gentlemen. I'll give you more pictures of it later to study and memorize, but this innocent old truck is reported to be hauling more than figs and dates. The number I was given was fifty million in US dollars."

"*Dat's* what I'm *talkin'* about!" said Jones. He leaned forward and whispered, "We get to keep a little taste?" He was grinning from ear to ear, his teeth white in contrast with very dark skin.

A stern look from Mackey was enough to shut him up, although he did exchange another wild handshake with Santos.

"While eleven of you take the field to play the Prince's Royal Team, Cascaes, Hodges, Jones, and Perez will be taking down the truck. Moose, you're pitching. And I am *ordering* you to throw a no-hitter while we run up the score."

That brought a few laughs. Mackey continued. "Listen, I wasn't given the whole scoop on this prince other than this— the guy's a multi-billionaire who loves American baseball. He just doesn't like Americans very much. He's got a domed stadium and brings in Minor League teams from the states for his own personal entertainment. While most of his buddies are buying and selling race horses, he's watching baseball or racing cars. It's my understanding that he has his own Royal Team from around the Middle East that trains with American coaches and players. Those are the guys you'll be playing. Who knows, maybe he'll own a team in the States in another year. In any event, the baseball game isn't why we're traveling halfway around the world. Fifty millions dollars is a large amount of money. I'm slightly concerned with our informant's information. According to our source, the money will not be guarded by more than two or three men to avoid suspicion at the border crossing. Let's hope that is correct."

Mackey changed slides and showed another map reference, depicting a road. "This point here is one of the most remote on the route from Riyadh to the border. The four of you will head out the night before in an unmarked truck. You'll take down the truck, transfer the money, and get back to Eskan by the time the game is over. We're supposed to play at ten hundred hours local time, so I want you back by noon, latest. You will have papers to get you back in Eskan Village with the civilian truck. We'll be back from the game by no later than thirteen hundred hours—hopefully earlier because Moose isn't going

to let them hit the ball, right Moose? Then we load the loot
and get out of Dodge before the Sheriff finds out there's been
a robbery."

Mackey paused, then added, "Oh, and don't get caught
stealing in Saudi Arabia. They'll cut off your hands before
they stone you to death." He flashed his own sarcastic smile at
Jones, who winced and looked down at his open hands.

Cascaes had been the SEAL team leader prior to the seven
of them being included in the baseball team. Although the
team didn't use their former ranks on a regular basis, Cascaes
was the senior man after Mackey and would be team leader for
the mission.

"The driver and guards?" asked Cascaes.

Mackey shook his head and made a slit-throat motion under
his own chin. "And I don't want them found, either," he added.

Cascaes nodded. "You say this area is remote. Not much
vehicle traffic?"

"Shouldn't be anybody out there. We're talking middle of
the desert." He pointed to Hodges, the Marine Sharpshooter.
"If any other vehicles approach the area, Hodges can give
them a flat tire before they get within a mile of our operation."

Hodges gave a quiet "Hooaa" to voice his enthusiasm about
shooting his newly-issued prototype sniper rifle.

Mackey continued. "We will have eyes in the sky to help
you locate the truck. Our guy inside Saudi has already placed a
GPS sensor on the vehicle, and it has been tracked ever since.
You'll get a heads-up when the target is getting close. This
shouldn't be too complicated."

Cascaes smiled. "They never are, until something gets
complicated."

"Yeah," Mackey grunted. "Chris, you and your crew will
work out the details on your own. The rest of you guys—
here's the lineup. Moose is throwin' a no-hitter. Ripper, you're
catching. Jake, first base…"

CHAPTER 6

Saudi Arabia

The jet landed in Riyadh, and the team walked out of the aircraft in their US Navy All-Star sweat suits. The Saudi Arabian weather welcomed them like a blowtorch with punishing sun and a cloudless sky. Their sweat suits were white with large blue stars running down the legs and arms. An American flag covered the left breast of the jacket with "All Stars" embroidered underneath. "US NAVY" was written across the back. The uniforms were flashy and professional looking, and the team looked every bit the part of an All-Star team. Each man carried a large duffle bag full of equipment, military uniforms, weapons, radios, and typical combat packs, as well as another duffle bag with their baseball uniforms, gloves, and batting helmets. They were prepared to play baseball or fight a small army.

The plane was greeted by an Air Force General who had been somewhat briefed by a member of the Joint Chiefs of Staff that this baseball team was to be treated as VIPs. Neither of the Generals knew anything about the actual mission, only that this team would be playing the prince's hand-picked baseball team at his personal indoor stadium. Simply put, the team was to have whatever they asked for, no questions asked—and that came straight from the Chairman of the Joint Chiefs himself. It was apparent to the Air Force General that greeted the plane that the President must have been a big baseball fan.

The General and his staff shook hands with Coach Mackey and his players and welcomed them to Saudi Arabia. He had one of his staff escort the team to a blue Air Force bus, where they stowed their gear and hopped aboard the air-conditioned bus to escape the desert heat. It had to be at least ninety-five degrees, and this was still spring. In another two months, it would be well over a hundred. The team politely listened to an Air Force sergeant tell them about the base, local customs, and where to find basic necessities. The bus pulled up in front of a four-story apartment building, which was immaculate and freshly painted in desert colors. The team unloaded and headed to their rooms, which were private—a nice surprise. They *were* VIPs, after all.

After they had unloaded, the team assembled in a small meeting room that had been reserved especially for them. Once there, the team helped Cascaes, Hodges, Jones, and Perez assemble their weapons and check their radios and gear. The game was to be played tomorrow morning, which meant the foursome working on the truck interception would be heading out tonight. It was already fifteen hundred hours, having lost a few in the air, and the men needed time to plan and then rest before heading out.

Once the weapons and radios were assembled, they were put back into their packs along with night vision equipment, body armor, Ghillie suits, some MREs, and water to last two days. The men changed into desert camos and pulled out maps to recheck their routes. In the meantime, Mackey arranged for a civilian truck to be brought to their apartment building, which would be the mode of transportation from Riyadh to the ambush point.

The team went back to their rooms, each with their own equipment, and tried to grab a couple of hours of sleep. At oh-three hundred, Cascaes and his crew headed down to the truck and took off for a small desert road to the north. At oh-six hundred, the rest of the team woke up and headed over to the chow hall to grab breakfast, now dressed in their brand new blue and white uniforms. They carried duffle bags that now held only baseball gloves, hats, and helmets, cleats, and batting gloves, and bats. (And micro-sized radios to communicate with their team.)

They were treated like star athletes in the dining hall, with other base personnel wishing them luck in 'kicking some Saudi ass.' The team smiled and shook hands with everyone, realizing that their uniforms did make them look like a team right out of the Majors. It was their first real game, and the men on the team where actually starting to get psyched about playing now that the crowd was egging them on. They had beaten every team they had played in Hawaii, most of them badly, but they had yet to play a *real* team.

None of them had really mentally prepared for baseball stardom. It was fun, but at the same time, they were trying to appear serious about the upcoming game. They did, in fact, want to win—it was their natural competitive spirit, but of course, they were all distracted by the mission that had started while they slept. They finished breakfast with lots of additional backslaps and high-signs, and they were happy to get out of there to a round of applause by the entire dining facility.

Coach Mackey smiled and waved as they left, and then quietly told his team to get their asses on the bus. They had a forty-minute drive by bus to the prince's private stadium.

While they all knew the man was stupid-rich, nothing could have prepared them for what they saw when they pulled into the stadium parking lot. It was a scaled down version of the Houston Astrodome. The stadium could hold 5,000 fans, although it was a private facility that rarely held more than three hundred. The stadium was domed and climate controlled, and the Astroturf field was as nice as anything in the Majors back home.

When the team arrived, their bus was greeted by a full staff of the prince's, who, they were told, was waiting for them inside. As they headed inside, a few of the players whistled quietly at the enormity of the stadium. Only a couple of the guys on the team had ever played college ball, and even those stadiums were nothing like this. There were electronic scoreboards and enormous replay screens—nicer than those found in most professional American stadiums.

The team followed their coach into the stadium and was greeted by Prince Abdul bin-Mustafa Awadi, their host. He was one of a few thousand billionaires in Saudi Arabia who smiled and did business with the west, while privately holding no love for the Americans outside of their one common interest—oil money. They went through the formalities and introductions but were surprised when an assistant came to the team and asked for each player's name, so they could be announced at the start of the game. That brought a few nervous chuckles.

When that business was settled, the team headed to their dugout by third base. They could see the opposing team enter their dugout from an inner door, and they watched them trot out onto the field where they began a formal warm up routine. Moose was the first to notice two of the players on the Saudi team. He grabbed Ripper, his catcher.

"Hey, Rip—you see who that *is* over there? That's Jose Torrez, man. Doesn't he play for the Mets?"

Ripper looked over and squinted. "Holy shit, man. You ain't kidding. Look who he's talking to."

Moose couldn't believe it. "Christ. That's Fernandez from Los Angeles. He hit like...three forty last year. You gotta be shittin' me."

"I guess when you're a billionaire, you can hire a guy to play one game," said Ripper. He looked back to Moose, but Moose was already trotting over to Mackey.

"Hey, Coach. We got problems with our little exhibition game," he said.

Mackey looked up from his roster. "What's up?"

"They've brought in ringers. That's Fernandez and Torrez over there."

Mackey raised his eyebrows. "That supposed to mean something to me?"

"Damn straight. Those guys are pros. They each made like a *boatload* of dough last year playing at home. Torrez throws like a hundred miles an hour, and Fernandez will be bouncing the ball off the lights. Lord knows what Prince Raghead paid these guys to play one game."

Mackey looked over at the Saudi team, in neat rows, stretching in pre-game warm-ups. Their white uniforms were immaculate. Only the beards on some of the players gave away their nationality—otherwise, they looked like a professional American team.

"Quit your bitching and get the guys out to do warm-ups like those guys. Try and look like a baseball team."

Smitty walked up to his Coach and whispered in his ear. "Problem, Coach."

"Yeah, I know about the ringers."

"Ringers?" asked Smitty.

"What's your problem, Smitty?"

"It's the radios. They are getting almost no signal in here. Must be the steel dome. I haven't been able to reach our team at all. Been trying since we walked in."

"Shit. Okay, keep at it. Oh, and be ready to play today. We may need your bat. The prince was kind enough to hire professional baseball players. Apparently, he takes this shit as seriously as I do."

Smitty looked across the field. "Holy crap. Isn't that Jose Torrez from the Mets?"

CHAPTER 7

Saudi Desert Road

Cascaes and his team had left in the dark, stopping only once at the front gate of Eskan to show papers and head off into the night. An hour outside of Riyadh, they turned off the main highway and headed off onto a narrow two-lane road that stretched through the flat dead earth. A few centuries of baking had turned everything the same shade of brown, although they couldn't see it in the dark.

Hodges was driving, his cheek full of chewing tobacco, while Cascaes watched their position on a laptop that sat where the name implied. Jones and Perez sat in the back and tried to catch a few Zs. Their truck, an unmarked, nondescript delivery box truck, rumbled along the dusty road alone in the Arabian night, following a path that had been used for a few centuries, but sometime during *this* one had finally gotten some asphalt. After about an hour on the narrow road, they climbed a small rise between two large rocky cliffs, a *pass* of sorts, and slowed down. As soon as they were over the rise, the truck slowly pulled off the road onto ground that was no softer than the asphalt.

"Wake up, sleeping beauties," said Cascaes to his rear seat passengers. "It's almost sunup. Time to start making ready for an armed robbery."

Jones stretched his legs and groaned, and Perez took a swig from his canteen.

"I wish this was coffee," he mumbled.

Hodges unpacked his Marine sniper rifle and pointed to the rocks overhead. Cascaes grunted, and Hodges took off to find himself a concealed spot to set up his ambush. Cascaes, Perez, and Jones pulled out their duffle bags, one of which contained dragon's teeth—metal spikes attached to a chain that could be laid across the road to blow the tires of their target. It could also be quickly yanked off the road if the wrong vehicle approached. Each of them had silenced automatic weapons with laser quick-sights. They took a tire from the back of the truck and leaned it against their vehicle. Anyone that might see them would assume they were simply fixing a flat. They were wearing civilian clothes and were not trying to pass as anything other than Americans traveling through Saudi on business, should the need to speak to anyone arise.

Cascaes and Perez stashed their weapons behind the spare tire and Jones took a position across the roadway, hidden in some rocks. The sun broke over the flat horizon to the east, spreading red and orange fingers through a dark sky. It would be the last sunrise for *somebody*.

Cascaes spoke on his hidden wrist mic to Hodges up in the rocks overhead. "You all set?"

"Roger that, Skipper. I can see y'all clear as a bell. Jones, I can see you picking your nose across the street."

Jones held up his middle finger. "Can you see what finger I'm holding up?" he asked quietly.

"That's very impolite," said Hodges quietly.

Cascaes ignored them and went over it one last time. "The truck hits the teeth and stops. Jonesy, you yank it as soon as they go over it so they don't see anything. They pull over and see us and assume we had the same problem. If they get antsy and make a move for weapons, Hodges, you whack 'em right away. Otherwise, we wait for them to pull over and get close enough to see how many there are. We hit them fast, unload the cash to our vehicle and bury the bodies. Jones and

Perez, you'll drive their vehicle back about a mile to that dry creek bed and ditch it out there. No one will find it for another thousand years. Everyone clear?"

Three quick "Rogers" answered him. "Hodges, how far down the road can you see from up there?"

"At least a mile and half, Skipper. Maybe more when the sun gets up higher."

"Okay, we'll wait for your heads up. We've got a few hours. Until then, you stay sharp. Jonesy, you stay out of sight. Out."

CHAPTER 8

Stadium

Mackey was shaking his head in disbelief. He wasn't exactly sure what he had expected, but it certainly wasn't this. The prince had an announcer introduce each player, his position on the field and batting average, in Arabic and English, from an unseen press box, and each team lined up on their appropriate baseline. "The Star Spangled Banner" was played, followed by the Saudi National Anthem. The Saudi players stood at attention as if they were going to be broadcast on national television, which, it turned out, they were. The Americans, realizing that this was more serious than they anticipated, imitated the Saudis, feeling intimidated for the first time since leaving basic training.

When the anthems were over, the teams went to their dugouts. The American team bombarded Mackey with questions and comments.

"Holy shit, Coach, this is nuts! We're gonna get killed," said Moose quietly.

"Bullshit," said Mackey, obviously irritated at the way things were starting out. "We came here to do a mission, which is what we're doing. You get to play baseball for a couple of hours. Don't embarrass us out there. And don't pitch to the ringer."

Moose was shaking his head. Mackey turned and addressed his team. "Okay, you guys, give the prince a game out there

27

today. You may actually have to do some fielding today for a change so pay attention. We're up in a minute, so watch their pitcher warm up. Take a few pitches and see what he's got. He may be throwing some heat out there. Jake, you're lead off."

Jake Koches had actually played baseball in college, but as he watched the pitcher hurl the ball at the catcher he cursed under his breath. The guy was a pro, with a fastball and a curve that was not like anything he'd seen other than on TV. He took a few practice cuts as he watched Jose Torrez throw a ninety-seven mile-per-hour fastball. He looked over at Mackey for sympathy, but Mackey was whispering to another player about communication problems. They were still getting static and hadn't spoken to Cascaes' team since they arrived at the stadium. As much as Mackey wanted to win the baseball game just to piss off the prince, it was actually irrelevant to the mission as long as they didn't get humiliated to the point that their team was obviously not an all-star team.

Mackey was concentrating on the radio when he heard the sound of a ball on leather and a loud *"Strike one!"* with an Arab accent. He looked up and watched Koches step out of the batter's box. The announcer was saying his name, but killing the pronunciation of Koches, making him sound Hebrew with the "ch" sound being a phlegm noise. Mackey cracked up at that.

Koches swung wildly at the next fastball as well.

"Strike two!"

"Jesus Christ!" yelled Mackey. "I told you guys to watch a few pitches first!"

"Strike three!"

Jake fought off the urge to throw his bat and trotted back to the dugout.

"What happened to *watching* a few pitches, Jake?" screamed Mackey.

"Coach, he threw three perfect strikes right down the middle."

"So why didn't you hit any of them if they were so perfect?" snapped Mackey.

"Because the motherfucker throws a hundred miles an hour!" he yelled, as he threw his batting helmet across the bench.

Pete McCoy, their shortstop and team speedster, was up second. After watching Jake get smoked, he made up his mind to bunt his way on. He took the first pitch, a called strike fastball, and smiled. He had barely *seen* the ball coming in.

"God *damn*, he throws *hard*," he said loud enough for the catcher to hear. The catcher smiled under his mask and signaled for his fifth consecutive fastball.

This time, Pete squared around as soon as the pitcher was finishing his motion and managed to get his bat on the ball. It bounced harder than he would have liked towards third, and he sprinted like a mad man. The catcher and third basemen almost collided, but the third basemen called him off and barehanded it, zipping it to first. Pete had managed to beat the ball to first, but he was wheezing, amazed at how hard the third basemen had thrown the ball. Who the hell *were* these guys?

Lance Woods, the resident surfer, walked out to the plate. Mackey wasn't really doing any coaching, as he was trying to get the damn radio to work, but he had signaled to McCoy, the fastest guy on the team, to steal. Woods would be swinging at the first pitch.

The guys on the bench were actually watching the game, even though they had no idea what was happening to their comrades out in the desert. They held their breath as Pete took a long lead. Torrez glanced in his direction but didn't think he would go and threw a slider to Woods, who actually got a piece of the ball by pure luck. The jump McCoy had gotten helped him get around second by the time the right fielder picked up the loping single, and McCoy burned it to third base.

Smitty walked out to the plate, rubbing dirt on his hands. He was strong as an ox, and even though he wasn't particularly tall or broad, he was just *hard*. His forearms and hands were anvils, and he was the best hitter on the team out of pure natural talent, even though he never played serious baseball before joining. When he got a hold of one, it *went*. The announcer called his name and number in a heavy Saudi accent.

"...and now batting for the Navy All-Stars, number seventeen, Joe Smith..."

The guys on the bench laughed. Smitty was CIA, and they figured his name was fake, but to hear "Joe Smith" announced on the stadium speakers made it all the more comical.

Torrez was trying to size him up, knowing he was the cleanup batter. He didn't like having men on first and third with one out, either. He had been paid a quarter of a million dollars and been given the most luxurious accommodations imaginable to pitch this game—but he had also guaranteed a win. He could feel the prince glaring from behind home plate in his special luxury box seat. McCoy and Woods were taking small leads and screaming at Smitty to hit one out of the park like a bunch of Little Leaguers. Even the guys on the bench were getting into it now, standing up at the dugout fence and yelling at their teammate, while Cory Stewart shushed them as he tried to listen to his earpiece for any communication with their ambush team.

"Strike one!" yelled the umpire as Smitty watched the first pitch break at the corner of the plate. He had never seen a professional curveball from the batter's box and found it somewhat amazing. His bat had never moved. He stepped out of the batter's box and looked around at the huge stadium. For a guy who'd been all over the world doing all kinds of Black Ops, he was a dumbfounded little kid. He stepped back in and took a deep breath, and Torrez threw a fastball that was a hair inside, brushing him back a little. Smitty was pissed, figuring this was no accident, and in his mind was already firing a three round burst into the pitcher's chest.

Torrez missed another one, and finally loaded up the count on Smitty, who still hadn't moved his bat yet. Finally. McCoy snapped him out of it.

"Hey, Smitty! You gonna look at that fucking thing all day? *Hit the fucking ball!*" he screamed from third base.

It was unprofessional, uncouth, and just what Smitty needed. The fastball came right down the middle, and Smitty crushed it over the center field wall. His teammates were standing on the bench screaming and hugging each other, and the prince stood up to applaud politely, a very fake smile on his face as he acknowledged Coach Mackey and the batter with a slight bow of his head. He sat and picked up a phone that rang in the Saudi dugout. As soon as the Saudi coach hung up the phone with the prince, he turned back to the field and started screaming at his players in Arabic. The catcher jogged out to speak to Torrez as Smitty was mobbed by his teammates in the dugout.

"I got 'em on the horn," whispered Cory Stewart to Mackey in the back of the dugout. "It's fuzzy, but they're in position waiting for the delivery."

Mackey nodded that he had heard and yelled some encouragement to Raul Santos as he jogged out to the plate, then looked up at the prince, delighted to see him so aggravated. "You're pissed now? Wait till you find out your truck got whacked," he thought to himself, assuming the prince was somehow connected to the fifty million.

Vinny Colgan, who they called Ripper, was walking up to the warm-up circle. He looked back at Mackey. "Hey, Coach, if we kick their ass, ya think they'll raise gas prices another buck?"

That got a few high fives from the now overconfident dugout that had yet to take the field.

CHAPTER 9

It was after ten hundred hours when Cascaes announced that the GPS locator was appearing on his laptop. He was looking at an aerial photograph with a GPS map overlay. A red dot appeared on the fringe of his screen, and every few seconds would move closer to the centered triangle that marked their position.

Hodges checked in from his location up in the rocks using his throat mic. He was in his Ghillie suit and prone on the rocky ledge with his sniper rifle set up on a bi-pod mount. "I have a visual. Truck is inbound, maybe two clicks."

"Roger that; positions everyone," said Cascaes quietly. Perez was using high-powered binoculars to scan the road in the opposite direction to make sure they didn't get any surprises from their rear. After a few minutes, Hodges was back on his throat mic. "Positive ID on the vehicle. It's a match to our truck."

"GPS confirms," said Cascaes.

Hodges chambered a round in his sniper rifle and looked down the road at the approaching vehicle. It was difficult to focus too clearly because the truck was bouncing as it approached in the dusty road with heat roils distorting his view, but he could make out three occupants on the vehicle's bench seat.

"I have a driver and two additional guys up front. Windshield is filthy. Can't tell if they're carrying weapons."

"Roger that," said Cascaes quietly. "Jones, when he hits the teeth, you yank 'em out of the road and get on the SAW. (M249 Squad Automatic Weapon—a heavy machine gun. At one hundred rounds per minute, it is capable of effective suppressing fire.) Weapons hold unless someone starts shooting."

Hodges whispered back every few seconds with the distance of the truck until they could hear it rumbling down the desert road towards them. It was still on the other side of the small rise, and only Hodges could actually see it. It was traveling at about fifty miles an hour, which probably seemed fast to the three occupants bouncing all over the road inside the ancient truck.

"Coming in now," said Hodges, a little more excitement in his voice this time. A second later, the truck came over the small rise and hit the dragon's teeth that lay across the road. The front and rear tires exploded and shredded into a million pieces, and Jones whipped the teeth off of the road to conceal them. The truck squealed and swerved as the driver fought to keep control of his truck. It was old and handled poorly enough with all *four* tires. Now it was on two, and the brakes were screaming as it fishtailed and slid up the road sideways not more than fifty yards from Cascaes and Perez, who knelt by a spare tire pretending to use a jack on their own vehicle.

The target truck finally came to rest in a cloud of dust, and at first no one moved. Hodges could look down at the dirty windshield, but he could hardly see through it.

"Skipper, looks like movement inside—one of them has a weapon," said Hodges calmly, his southern drawl always more hidden when he was totally focused.

Cascaes stood with his hands on his hips, staring at his truck and then theirs, putting on an Academy Award performance as "the man with the busted truck." He spoke into his concealed throat mic to his team.

"Just cover me. Don't shoot unless you have to."

Cascaes walked towards the vehicle. And the driver opened his door and began shouting in Arabic. Cascaes continued walking towards him, speaking back in English about the lousy road and his flat tire. The man was growing more agitated and reached back into the truck, where one of his passengers handed him an AK47.

"*Weapon!*" said Hodges. "I'm taking the shot!"

The rest happened in an instant. A single round traveled from Hodges' sniper rifle exploding through the windshield, which spider-webbed, blocking Hodges' view of the inside of the truck, and then through the man's skull, which exploded. Cascaes hit the deck and yelled, "Cover fire!"

Perez fired a few bursts at the cab with his MP5 as Hodges fired a second .338 Lapua round through the dusty glass. A cloud of blood splattered against the inside of the glass. Jones opened up with the SAW over Chris' head, putting hundreds of rounds through the cabin of the truck as Chris rolled over and over to the side of the road to find cover.

Hodges called down to cease fire, and everything stopped. It was silent again in the desert, except for the sound of the hissing, dying engine that had a few hundred rounds lodged in it from the SAW. Glass fell with a plink against the hard road. A second later, a body fell out of the cabin. It was the driver, or what was left of him. Perez ran up the road calling Chris on his mic.

"Skipper, you in one piece?"

Chris sat up and looked at the smoking truck. "Yeah, I'm good. Jones? Hodges?"

They both called back that they were fine. Perez and Cascaes ran to the truck and looked inside. They both were shocked to see two young boys lying awkwardly on the bench seat, their heads and bodies blown open. The driver did have an AK47, but that was the only weapon in the truck.

"Fuck!" said Cascaes out loud. He and Perez stood, stunned at the sight of the two kids.

"What is it Skipper?" asked Hodges from overhead.

"They're fucking *kids*!" said Cascaes loudly. There was no reason to check for pulses, they each had been hit a few dozen times, including headshots that had torn them up pretty badly.

"Oh Jesus," said Perez, crossing himself. "Is this even the right fuckin' truck?"

Jones ran to them from his position, carrying the smoking SAW. When he saw the grisly mess inside the cabin, he abruptly turned and vomited. He started crying and knelt down in the middle of the road.

"Oh, God! Oh, my *God*! I just murdered two little *kids*!" He was on all fours, wailing.

Hodges checked in every direction, and when he saw it was clear, he started to scramble down from the rocks. Cascaes saw him move and yelled back to him.

"Stay where you are! Keep your eyes open up there—both directions. Jones, get your shit together and help me search this truck. The GPS tracker was on the vehicle, this *has* to be it!" He was praying to himself that it *was*.

Perez had already started to head around to the back of the truck and opened the doors carefully, his weapon at the ready. There were dozens of boxes of dates, which he started pulling out onto the road. He tore through the first couple of boxes, which contained only fruit.

"Shit!" he screamed as he ripped open box after box as fast as he could, a cold dreadful feeling in the pit of his stomach. Was this the right truck? The sunlight streamed into the back through hundreds of bullet holes, the light hazy in the smoky air. Cascaes hopped up into the truck with Jones following behind, his face still wet with tears.

Chris started throwing boxes to Perez and Jones, who stacked them neatly in the road as they checked each one and found only dates. They had calmed down a bit and realized that they would have to reload the truck, so they were slower and more methodical now. Cascaes threw down the last box.

"That's it!" he yelled.

"There's nothing here, Skipper, just fucking prunes!" yelled Jones.

"They're dates, idiot," said Perez, his mouth full of them.

"Hodges, how we doing?" asked Chris.

"Clean and green, Skipper."

Perez ran back to the cab and started looking under the bloody shot-up seat. Cascaes called him back. "Perez, we're looking for fifty million dollars! It ain't gonna be in the fucking glove compartment!"

Cascaes stood in the back of the now empty truck, hands on his hips, totally pissed. "I can't fucking *believe* this," he screamed at no one in particular.

Hodges called down on his mic. "Hey, Skipper, were they really kids?"

"Shut up," he answered quietly.

Jones was fighting back tears again looking at the wooden planks of the truck that Chris was standing on. One of them was sticking up a little bit, the end chewed up from bullets.

He pulled himself up into the truck and gently pushed Chris a drop to his left, then started pulling up the floorboard. There was something under it. As soon as Chris realized what Jones was doing, he dropped to his knees and pulled out his K-Bar knife. The two of them worked together, prying up the splintered board.

"Ernie," yelled Chris to Perez, "get me that crowbar!"

Perez took off in a flash, while Chris and Jones continued ripping up the floor. The board snapped off, exposing a square brick wrapped in newspaper. They pulled it out and tore off a corner of the paper. American hundred dollar bills were neatly stacked in a little brick of money.

"Sonofabitch," said Cascaes softly.

"Leave it to the brutha' to find the quan, man," said Jones quietly. He was trying to be cool, but he couldn't get the image of the two young boys blown to pieces all over the front seat out of his head. He must have personally put a hundred rounds through them. His blank expression echoed the empty feeling in his chest.

Perez returned with the crowbar and whistled as he saw the brick of money in Cascaes' hand. "*Damn*, man. They had it stashed in the floor," he said out loud but to himself.

"Jones found it. Get up here and let's get this stuff loaded into our truck. We gotta hustle."

It took fifteen solid minutes of grunting and groaning to rip up the entire floor. When they were finished, they had over a hundred of the heavy paper bricks stacked on the ground next to the dates. Cascaes ran down the road and hopped into their truck, letting the spare roll off the road, and raced back to the rear of the other truck. Jones, now with his shirt off and his dark muscled body dripping wet, was quick to start throwing bricks into the back of their truck. They loaded up quickly, and Chris hopped out to help reload the dates into the back of the other truck.

Perez hopped up onto the running board of the truck, trying not to touch the mangled bodies that were still leaking blood. He tried the engine, but it was totally dead, with more bullet holes in it than the two dead bodies inside the cab. He cursed and hopped down, grabbing the driver and hoisting him up into the cab with the two young kids. He ran back to Chris, wiping his bloody hands on his pants.

"Skipper! The truck is totally dead. Now what?"

Cascaes wiped his sweaty forehead. "Shit. This wasn't part of the simple plan. I'll try and push it with our truck, but it's only on two wheels. I dunno if this is going to work or not. Let's get it off the road into those rocks if we can. Maybe it will go unnoticed at least till we're out of Saudi. Get behind the wheel and try and aim it towards that depression off the road."

"What about them?" asked Perez.

"Leave them in the cab. There must be a million rounds in this truck and all over the road—hiding the bodies isn't going to fool anybody."

Perez jogged back to the cab and looked in. Flies had already materialized out of thin air. Blood and hunks of flesh and brain were splattered everywhere. There was no way he was sitting in the driver's seat, so he stood on the running board with the door open while Cascaes drove his truck slowly into position behind the dead vehicle.

The two trucks groaned with the sound of metal on metal as Cascaes slowly eased into the rear of the fifty million dollar fruit truck. Perez cranked the wheel with the gears in neutral as Cascaes used first gear to push. Sparks flew off the bare metal rim of the front wheel, and the last pieces of rubber fell off the back tire as the truck slowly inched forward. Perez fought the wheel as the truck turned off the road and picked up some momentum.

The truck slid into a small depression off the road and stopped moving. Cascaes gave it more gas, but it was no good and the tires on his truck began to spin and smoke. He could smell burning rubber. He gave up and backed away from the truck, yelling for Perez to get back to their own vehicle. Jones ran to their truck and Cascaes called to Hodges to rejoin the group. As Hodges made his way down, Chris went to his duffle bag and pulled out a white phosphorous grenade. When Hodges arrived, Cascaes told everyone to get into their truck, which he had turned in the direction of Eskan Village. He walked down to the cab of the other truck and tossed the live grenade into it, then sprinted back to his own vehicle down the road. The cab exploded in a huge fireball and burned wildly. By the time anyone found it, there wouldn't be much of anything except some burnt metal.

He hopped into his own truck and gunned the engine. As they peeled off for Eskan, he told Hodges to try and call Mackey. Hodges did as he was told but, as happened earlier in the day, there was no signal. Jones craned his neck and watched the burning truck getting smaller in the distance. He fought the wave of nausea in the pit of his stomach as it exploded again, giving him one final stab into his heart.

CHAPTER 10

What had gotten off to a great start only lasted until the Saudi team came up to bat in the bottom of the first inning. Moose was throwing hard, but by the end of the first inning it was three to three. By the end of the fifth, they were losing seven to four. Now, top of the ninth, they were getting ready for their last attempt to come up with three runs.

Moose was the lead-off hitter, and he was exhausted. He had pitched the whole game, not expecting to be facing professionals. They had pretty much shelled him all day. And he had been throwing as hard as he possibly could. This was finally his chance to get some revenge.

No such luck. Torrez threw him curves, sliders, and finally struck him out with a knuckle ball that seemed to dance around in front of him before passing his huge swing. Moose surprised his teammates by giving the opposing pitcher a tip of his hat after he struck out. This guy was the real deal, and Moose knew he had been totally outclassed. Of course, Moose was a Navy SEAL, and he wasn't getting paid millions of dollars a year to throw baseballs, either.

Top of the lineup again—Koches was up. He had struck out twice, flied out once and gotten a single. He walked out to the plate and tapped his cleats with his bat like he had seen the pros do growing up. He spit, again, for no particular reason and did his best to look menacing for the pitcher who had been killing him all day.

"Strike one!"

40

He stepped out, took a practice swing, and smiled broadly; then he looked back at the dugout. He mouthed the words "fuck 'em" to his teammates, and then did his best Babe Ruth impersonation by pointing to the center-left alley. He teammates screamed encouragement, fired up by his bravado.

"Strike two!"

He stepped out of the box again, now really pissed after almost knocking himself over with the last swing. Then he remembered his college coach at Rutgers. "Don't try and kill it on a fastball pitcher—just get a piece and it will go…"

Torrez, getting tired after pitching the whole game, something he hadn't done in six years, and being made to throw a lot more pitches than he had anticipated, did his best to throw a fastball. He was throwing in the low eighties now, and Koches was able to get his bat on the ball with a solid line drive that bounced off the wall and got him to second base. His team was screaming and standing up in the dugout. Torrez wiped his brow and kicked the dirt. He had been quite sure he was going to throw a no-hitter against these Navy clowns.

McCoy was up next, and had been having a pretty good day with a bunt to start things off for their first rally, then a walk and two singles. Torrez threw him some chin music to back him up, but McCoy was a SEAL and not easily intimidated. The next pitch was a fastball, probably the slowest one of the day as Torrez grew more tired, and McCoy got all of it. He had never been a power hitter, but this sucker was *gone*, clear over the right field fence. Seven to six, with their best hitters coming up. The prince was back on the phone to the Saudi dugout, giving very calm, quiet death threats.

Woods walked out to the plate and smiled up at the prince, who did not return the smile. He stepped into the batter's box. In the dugout, Mackey's earpiece finally came on.

"Mack, you read me?" It was Cascaes, sounding a little tense with lots of background noise and static.

"I read you," he said quietly into his wrist mic as nonchalantly as possible. "Where the hell ya been?"

"Ball one!"

"We are almost back at Eskan with the fruit. It was not as simple as planned."

Mackey grimaced. "Everyone okay?"

"Roger that. I'll brief you when I see you, but we need to move up our exit, like *pronto*."

"Roger. We'll get back ASAP. Out." Mackey casually turned to Smitty as Woods ripped one over the shortstop's head for a single. He grabbed Smitty's arm as he was heading out of the dugout. "Strike out as fast as possible and we're outta here, you understand?"

"Are you shittin' me, Boss? Lance is the tying run…"

"Strike out and we're *out* of here. That's a *direct order*." He turned to his team and quietly spread the word. "As soon as he strikes out, get your shit together and we need to double time it back to Eskan. Act pissed off so the prince thinks we're sore losers and understands why we won't stay for dinner and shit. We need to hustle."

His players hated to lose, but they understood that they weren't here to play baseball. Smitty jogged out to the plate and Lance started screaming some encouragement from first base. Smitty ignored the urge to try and kill it and swung at the first pitch, which was in the dirt. The second pitch was also wild, and again he swung and missed. He could feel the prince's smile behind him and wanted to open up his royal head with the bat, but instead he pounded the plate and swung wildly at the third pitch. He threw his bat and walked back towards the dugout as the catcher ran out to the mound to congratulate his exhausted pitcher.

Lance jogged over to Smitty, annoyed. "What the fuck were you swinging at, man?"

"Shut up—we're outta here, boss's orders," he sneered back. Damn, he hated striking out on purpose.

The few friends of the prince stood and clapped, and the announcer came on with the final statistics. Coach Mackey stepped out onto the field and saluted the prince politely, then turned to his players. "Everybody get your ass to the bus."

They headed out the same way they came in but were stopped by one of the prince's men. "His eminence invites you to dine with him and his team, after you help yourselves to our shower facilities and locker room…"

Mackey gave a fake smile and replied tersely, "Please, tell the prince that my men are sore losers and will be heading back to base to be yelled at by their coach for a few hours." He walked past him somewhat brusquely, followed by his sweaty, pissed off team in the direction of their waiting bus.

CHAPTER 11

Eskan Village

The bus pulled into Eskan after a quiet ride back. The mission wasn't discussed on the bus. Instead, the players discussed the game. Although they were angry about losing, they could live with the fact that they had held their own against a bunch of ringers. Much of the conversation was about the stadium itself. They were all pretty amazed that one person could build a multi-million dollar facility for his own personal use a couple of times a year. They all agreed the lavish expense was the reason gas was over three dollars a gallon.

The bus stopped in front of their neat little housing unit, where a plain looking truck sat parked out front. Jones was sitting in the open back of the truck with his SAW across his lap. Perez paced around the front with his MP5 strapped across his chest, and Hodges sat in the cab, engine running. They were simply guarding the truck while Cascaes was upstairs packing up all of their gear so they'd be ready to hustle when the team arrived.

Hodges spoke into his mic from inside the truck cab to Cascaes. "Skipper, the team's back."

"Roger that," said Chris, who walked out to the parking lot to greet the team, two large duffle bags slung over his back.

The bus squealed to a stop, the airbrakes hissing, and the team walked down the steps, still in their cleats and dirty baseball uniforms. The two Chrises shook hands, and Cascaes spoke first. "I've got a plane on the runway, gassed up and ready to go. The fruit truck was as described, except there were two little kids aboard with the driver to throw off the border guards."

"And?" asked Mackey.

"We didn't know. Not that we could have done anything differently anyway. We would have been made for Americans if we'd left them alive. Anyway, Jones and Perez were kind of shaken up. All of us, I guess. Let's just get the fuck out of here before someone finds the truck. I had to burn it. We couldn't ditch it like we planned—it was too shot up."

"Simple plan, huh?" said Mackey quietly. He turned back towards the bus and yelled, "Hey! Hold up! We're getting back on." He jogged over to the bus and stuck his head back inside. "We need to get over to the airfield *pronto*."

"You're leaving now, sir?" asked the young airman driving the bus.

"Right now." He looked back at his team that had just gotten off the bus and yelled over to them. "Everyone back on board. Hodges, Perez, and Jones—you too. I'll ride with Cascaes. You can shower in Germany."

He jogged over to the truck and let Cascaes drive, following the bus through the neat little streets of Eskan Village back to the airfield where their transport plane would be waiting. They would connect in Germany to refuel and change crews, then straight to Virginia, where people above their pay grade would decide what happened to the fifty million dollars sitting in eight large duffle bags in the back of their truck. Cascaes told Mackey everything that happened from beginning to end, and when he was finished, Mackey told him about the baseball game—a far more pleasant story than shooting two kids to death.

CHAPTER 12

They had showered and changed clothes at a US Airbase in Germany, then reboarded their transport plane to try and get some sleep in uncomfortable seats. Jones woke up somewhere over the Atlantic in a cold sweat, the mutilated faces of the two boys splattered all over the front seat in his nightmare. He woke Perez out of a dead sleep.

Ernesto Perez, simply known as "Ernie P." woke up startled, automatically reaching for his gun that wasn't there. He blinked a few times and looked around the dark aircraft before he remembered where he was. He looked at Earl Jones, who looked like he had just seen a ghost, because Jones was pretty sure he *had*. His face was covered in sweat.

Perez whispered, "Wussup?"

Jones whispered back over the low drone of the plane. "Nightmares, man. I keep seeing those kids in the truck. I blew the shit out of two little *kids*, man." Jones was literally shaking in his seat.

"Holmes, it wasn't our fault, man. The dude grabbed his gun and was gonna shoot Mack. What the fuck was he thinkin', anyway? Bringin' two little kids with him to smuggle money to terrorists…it was fucked up, man, but it wasn't our fault. I fired at the truck, too, man, and so did Hodges. That shit ain't on us, man. It's on the dude that brought the kids. Take a deep breath and get some sleep, you look like shit."

Earl leaned back and tried to close his eyes, but every time he did, he could feel the tears coming. It was right in front of

46

him—two little kids on the front seat, their mutilated bodies, and the blood running out of the truck onto the dusty road... he stared at the dark ceiling until troubled sleep finally came.

Ernie looked over at him every hour or so to see if he was sleeping, his own sleep now ruined by the same nightmare. He was fearless and had seen plenty of killing, including dead civilians in Iraq and Afghanistan—but had never killed a civilian himself. He exhaled slowly and fought back his own tears in the dark cabin.

⊕

The team touched down in Virginia near CIA headquarters at eleven in the morning, almost thirty hours after stealing fifty million dollars of terrorist money. The tires bounced on the tarmac with a short screech, and the plane taxied to the end of the runway. They were at a private airfield owned by the CIA, just outside of Langley. A black bus was at one end of the runway, escorted by a black SUV. The rear of the aircraft opened and the ramp lowered to allow the team out with all of their gear, including heavy duffle bags filled with bricks of American hundreds.

After several months of rigorous training at another facility, and now their first mission successfully under their belt, they were finally going to meet "the boss," Dex Murphy at the official home of CIA's Special Operations Training Center. They were now officially "on the inside."

Dex Murphy opened the door of the SUV and stepped out. He walked over to greet his old friend Chris Mackey, who introduced him to Chief Petty Officer Christopher Cascaes, team leader of the six SEALs now imbedded with the baseball team. The rest of the team headed for the black bus, still jet lagged, while Mackey and Cascaes hopped into the back of the SUV behind Dex and his driver. The team would be housed at CIA's training facility near headquarters. They made

some small talk in the truck as they headed through security
gates and a corridor of barbed wire, cameras, and guard
towers. Eventually, they arrived at the housing facility where
hundreds of agents were housed, trained, drilled, and schooled
in hundreds of different specialties and spy craft which would
hopefully keep them alive in a hostile world.

The two vehicles pulled in front of the small buildings and
everyone piled out, still dragging all of their gear. The money
was shoved into the rear of the SUV and everyone was given
three hours to shower, relax, and grab some food before a
major debriefing inside the fortress-like building. Dex offered
them a "welcome home" as they walked to the building, weary
from a *very* long week.

Dex stood with Chris Mackey and Chris Cascaes, his arms
folded across his chest as he watched the team walk into the
building. He shook his head and half-smiled. "Mac, in all the
years I've been doing this, this has to be the wackiest ensemble
of personnel to ever step into that building. We've got military
personnel from damn near every branch of the service on your
little baseball team. It's just plain old bizarre."

Mackey smiled. "I know. But I tell you what—it worked.
You know I've been around the block a few times myself, Dex.
These guys are naturals. Natural athletes, trained warriors,
and street smart—they've got it all. They work together like
they've been doing it all their lives. We add some spy craft
to their resumes and we're going to have a serious little army
in there. That baseball team could take down some small
countries all by themselves."

Dex looked at him without smiling. "Good. Because they
may have to." Dex paused thoughtfully and leaned forward
to speak in a softer voice. "Mack, we go back a long way.
I have to tell you, things are changing around here. Darren
Davis is a good guy and he tries to have my back, but the new
Commander in Chief has his own peeps he wants in the chain
of command. Davis is getting heat from the President's hand-

selected bullshit artist, Randall Hill. Your team's cover gets blown or something goes south, it'll be more than just *you* looking for a new job. Right after they throw all of you out the front door, they'll push me out the back."

Mackey scowled. "Dex, you should be running this whole damn building; what the hell are you talking about?"

"What have you done for me lately, know what I mean? I've given twenty years to this place, and the last six months they've been talking to me like I just started my probationary period. I love my agents and the folks in the building, but the politics is getting real old. I'll leave when I'm ready, not because some suit who's in way over his head wants me out."

"Roger that," said Mack.

"Anyway, your guys proved Hill wrong already. Just keep doing what you're trained to do. Hill is my problem. I just wanted you to know that there are people on our side that wouldn't mind seeing you fail, for no other reason than to get rid of me." Dex smacked Mackey on the shoulder and walked away towards the building, with Cascaes and Mackey exchanging glances and following close behind.

CHAPTER 13

CIA Training Facility

The team had showered and changed into plain gray sweat suits. Had they gone outside to run the confidence course, they would have looked like everyone else out there, except they would probably shave a few minutes off the fastest times. They reassembled in a large conference room and took seats at a long rectangular table. Dexter Murphy had been at the door and personally shook hands and greeted each man as he came in. When they were all seated, he took his seat at the head of the table.

"Gentlemen, on behalf of Director Wallace Holstrum, I'd like to officially welcome you to the Central Intelligence Agency. You've all signed your lives away more than once prior to joining this team, but let me just remind you that everything you see, hear, and do while at this facility is highly classified information. Keeping a secret is one of the hardest things for a human being to do. However, when secrets are blown in *our* world, people die.

"Your personnel records have been changed to reflect special reassignment to Navy Intelligence; however, you will also have new personnel records kept here and only here. While I know you aren't in this for the money, you will be happy to know that you will be paid by this agency for your time with us, over and above your military pay.

"You are, to my knowledge, the largest team we have ever used in this manner. Our operations are covert and usually performed by single agents or very small teams. Two and three man units, typically. While we occasionally have operatives imbedded with larger military groups, we have never had this many agents working together in the field. You're appearing together, in public, on a regular basis. It's highly irregular and very dangerous and, quite frankly, makes me uncomfortable. That said, your first job went surprisingly well."

Jones mumbled to himself, "Yeah, fuckin' great."

Dex heard the comment and didn't let it pass. "Mr. Jones, I understand your feelings about the unfortunate deaths of the two children on that truck." Jones eyes snapped to his, surprised that he knew everything already. "The fifty million dollars that you intercepted will save countless numbers of other children in Iraq or Afghanistan or wherever the hell that money was going, as well as American lives and coalition forces. Until those countries are stabilized, children will continue to die there *every day*. You all did your part to prevent some of that bloodshed. Fifty million dollars buys explosives and weapons, intelligence and bribes. The Iraqis are holding their government together by a shoestring. Don't underestimate the importance of what you did."

Jones looked down at his hands, folded on the table. He could still see the bodies leaking blood all over the truck.

"A team the size of yours has specific uses in the war on terror. With your advanced training and conditioning, your baseball team is as effective as a small army. Mercenary companies like Executive Outcomes fought in Angola and Sierra Leone against tens of thousands of soldiers, without much more manpower than you have here at this table. That said, you *do* need some additional training. Not with your military skills—we all know you can fight. And the reports I read from your previous training and mission prep were all outstanding. But the types of operations that you will be conducting will require specialty skills that not all of you have been exposed to. This is why you have been brought here.

"Over the next six weeks, you will be taught to use 'toys' that you have never seen before. We have surveillance equipment, weapons, computer, and satellite systems available to you that you will need to train on to maximize their effectiveness in the field. For the first five weeks you will train with new equipment and spend some time with agency instructors. The sixth week will be mission specific, and then you will be redeployed.

"Frankly, gentlemen, you're all one big experiment. SEALs, Marine Recondos, Army Rangers, and our own personnel working together would have been inconceivable only a few years ago, but the battle space has changed, the enemy has changed, and the times have changed. We are going to use every means available to us to keep our nation safe, which translates to thinking outside the box. You, gentlemen, are outside the box."

"The batter's box," said Ernie quietly.

Dex smiled. "We'll use the baseball team as a cover for as long as we think it's safe. At some point, we may need to change your cover story—either a little, or completely, but that will depend on circumstance. In the meantime, check your egos at the door and try and learn as much as you can from our instructors. You're going back to war gentlemen, just in a way you've never done before."

Dex stood up. "I'll show you where you can grab some lunch, then it's off to class for all of you except Mackey and Cascaes. We're going to see Darren Davis."

CHAPTER 14

CIA Training Facility

Dex led Mack and Chris to another conference room and showed them to the coffee machine on a side table. Coffee—the lifeblood of the military and CIA.

They sat at one end of a long mahogany table and Dex pressed an intercom button on the table. He spoke briefly to someone named Kim, who arrived a moment later with a laptop under one arm and a coffee cup in her other hand. She had the brisk, no-nonsense walk of a woman used to working in a man's world.

"Gentlemen, meet Kim Elton. Kim is the assistant desk chief for the Gulf States. Basically, she covers Kuwait, Bahrain, Qatar, the UAE, Oman, and Yemen. Don't let her big blue eyes fool you; she speaks fluent Arabic, French, some Hebrew, and a little Farsi for good measure. Kim, this is Chris and the other Chris."

She smiled and shook hands with the two men. "Excellent. I can't screw up your names."

"Actually, I go by Mack to make it more confusing on purpose."

"Nice," she replied, taking her seat and opening her laptop. She looked at Dex, who gestured for her to begin her briefing. Kim began typing and opened up a map of the Middle East. "Your team is cleared for confidential and secret clearances.

The two of you are cleared for Top Secret. This briefing is more informational in nature, but it does contain some confidential information."

"In other words, it's like everything else around here—keep your mouths shut," said Dex with a smile. "It's okay, Kim, I've already read them the riot act about secrecy."

"Yes, sir," she replied curtly. She was just reciting the required rigmarole. "In your original briefing, you had been told that the money you intercepted was heading to Iraq. We now believe that was incorrect. Today's focus in on Qatar. We've been getting some chatter and, on more than one occasion, Doha came up."

"Been there," said Cascaes. "The naval base."

"Naval base and a large air base. The Air Force runs a ton of missions to Afghanistan from Doha. The Al Udeid Air Base is home to both the US and Air Force Central Command and the 379th Air Expeditionary Wing. Plenty of F16s, J-Stars, KC tankers, and the Moon Dogs run electronic warfare from Al Udeid, as well. We're worried that it may be a terrorist target."

"I'm pretty sure the whole Middle East is a target," said Mackey.

"No doubt, there are plenty of targets. But Doha was specifically mentioned. We just don't know what or when. The security details on both bases have been notified, and blast walls are being constructed at Al Udeid. We believe the fifty million you intercepted was part of this."

"So if we got the money, doesn't that screw up their plans?" asked Cascaes.

"Fifty million is a lot of money in almost every part of the world except the Middle East. I'm sure you disrupted their plans, but if the money did, in fact, come from Prince Abdul bin-Mustafa Awadi, he'll have another fifty million tomorrow."

"So the prince is involved in all this? Why didn't we just cap him when we were there?" asked Cascaes, visibly annoyed.

"Assassinating foreign princes is frowned upon," said Dex quietly. "Unless we have absolute proof of his involvement, there's no touching him."

"Have the higher-ups talked to the Qataris?" asked Mackey.

Kim smiled and sat back, folding her arms. "Well, this brings us to the interesting part of the briefing. Qatar has a new emir. Sheikh Tamim bin Hamad Al Bahani—youngest leader in the Middle East. And he's a total contradiction, just like Prince Awadi, but we'll come back to Awadi in a second."

Kim keyed her computer and brought up a photograph of the emir. "Sheikh Bahani took over for his father last year. He's a very pragmatic businessman, and deals with the US, France, and Great Britain like an old friend. Qatar has a huge natural gas reserve as well as oil, and the highest per capita income in the world. He gives us the air base for free and loves having our forces there for his country's own security. Up until recently, they didn't even have their own air force. Anyway, this emir talks the talk and openly courts western business. He's also a huge soccer fan and had a huge stadium built for world soccer events."

"So we got a prince that loves baseball and an emir that digs soccer. Any Pashas over there like football? I'd like some seats on the fifty if you can work it out," mumbled Mackey.

Cascaes ignored him. "So this emir, he's one of the good guys?" asked Cascaes.

"I'm not finished," she said with a smile. "So, while he's being Mr. Friendly Businessman, he's also openly supporting the Muslim Brotherhood, Hamas, and Hezbollah. We believe he funnels money to all of them. He also tells his own people that he supports Sharia Law, *but* it's one of the only countries in the Middle East that allows pork and alcohol in designated areas. I'd bet a hundred bucks he drinks the world's best wine and champagne in his palace with his two wives when no one's looking. Now, while he's telling his clerics he's old school, he also changed the law and allowed women the right to vote and hold public office. Except, no woman holds public office because he appoints everyone, usually his family members. And, while he keeps talking about open elections and a new system of lawmaking, everything has to be approved directly by him, anyway. Basically, he tries to sound like his country is making progress, but he is very happy to live in a medieval society where the king makes all the rules, women are property, and he answers to no one."

"You weren't kidding about the contradiction part," said Cascaes.

"No, and Awadi is cut from the same cloth. Prince Abdul went to Princeton University to get his western education ten years ago. He becomes a huge baseball fan, and being the zillionaire that he is, he buys box seats to the Mets for his four years at college. You've played in his personal domed stadium—you see how fanatical he is about the game. Anyway, when he was in college, he'd take his new buddies to all the games by stretch limo. He totally loved being surrounded by the celebrities that have those kind of seats. He's drinking beer, eating hotdogs that he knows aren't one hundred percent beef, getting laid—a regular westerner. Except then he goes home, goes full-blown Sharia Law on everyone and marries three wives, pumps out nine kids that he doesn't see because he has the boys in the madras and the girls home in burqas. He's just like the emir—do as I say, not as I do. So while he's selling oil and gas to the Americans and talking baseball, he's also very content to see America and Israel annihilated."

"I think I'm noticing a pattern," said Cascaes sarcastically.

"Ya think?" added Mackey.

Kim continued, "So, we believe that the prince is financing operations with various terrorist groups, possibly with the knowledge of the emir. We don't think the emir would be happy about an attack on the air base, but if it *did* happen and killed some Americans, he wouldn't lose sleep over it either."

"Hey, I've got an idea," said Cascaes.

"Yeah?" asked Dex.

"How about we use our planes at the airbase there and carpet bomb the whole fucking country."

"I do not believe that would be considered good foreign policy by the current administration," said Dex.

"It's ridiculous," said Cascaes.

"Typical Middle Eastern mentality, I'm afraid," said Kim. "The enemy of my enemy is my friend. And they all change friends and enemies pretty routinely. We're there because of three reasons: location, location, location. We like the base on the Gulf. We do business with them because we need the gas and oil. But we're also well aware that their banking system is allowing money to be funneled to terrorist organizations and they won't make any attempts to stop it. We use them, they use us. It is what it is."

"Yeah, well, it's *bullshit* is what it is," said Cascaes. "Pardon my French."

"I speak French. I don't believe I recognized your dialect," said Kim with a smile. "Anyway, welcome to the Middle East. Nothing is as it appears. And in the case of these two, I'm not sure *they* even know when they're lying."

"When their mouths are moving," replied Mackey.

"Pretty much," said Dex. "I just wanted to give you an idea of what you're dealing with."

"Yeah, well that cleared it right up, thanks," said Cascaes. He thought for a moment. "Awadi's in Saudi. You said the Qatari Sheikh knows that the prince is funding terrorists, but he's in Qatar? What's the connection between these two?"

"Money," said Kim. The Saudis and Qataris share some of the oil and gas fields along their mutual border. They're both basically drilling down into the same giant pocket of gas. It's sensitive, so they play nice together. Prince Awadi owns thousands of acres of desert along the Qatar border. He and the emir have regular communication, and there's been money exchanged between the two of them for many years, although it isn't clear why. Most likely, just land leases."

"I still don't get it. How does their mutual oil business have anything to do with the prince's interest in funding terrorists?" asked Chris.

"My guess is, they have an arrangement to make sure they don't have any conflicts. If the prince funds an attack that hits a gas pipeline or blows up some petro facility, it better not be the emir's property that gets hit."

"That's nice," said Mackey. *"You can blow up whatever you want—just make sure it isn't my stuff."*

"Sounds just about right," replied Kim. "It's also about keeping their governments stable so they can pump oil unmolested. When the hard liners get strong, then they have to allow some Anti-Western muscle flexing. When the moderates are strong, they have to look very professional and first world. The mood changes with the prevailing wind over there. To stay in power, the government has to play to a lot of different factions at the same time."

CHAPTER 15

Tariq walked through the loud, crowded market street in an ancient section of the city, southwest of Riyadh. The dusty streets were packed with merchants and their customers, children and beggars, goats and dogs. He pushed his way through the hot, narrow street towards the address he had been given. Crates of chickens were stacked six feet high, and they squawked and clucked incessantly. Spice merchants mixed their secret concoctions and swapped brown bags of spices and herbs for cash with women in burqas. The spices, chickens, goats, and sweaty people combined to create a very special local perfume. It was a busy day.

He stopped and looked up at a building, wondering if he was at the correct address. The buildings and streets were all almost the same color, blending into an endless maze of non-descript light brown that was only broken up by an occasional painted door or sign. A large hand squeezed his bicep and a gruff voice said, "Come." Tariq was then guided through the crowd with a large man on each side of him, moving him quickly down small side alleys. There was another man behind them, and they walked faster than was comfortable through the crowd. Tariq was again pulled down a side alleyway where a small car was waiting. The car took up almost the entire width of the street, and Tariq was told to get into the back seat. The other three men got in and started the car with a cough of black smoke, and then began moving through the labyrinth of streets as they headed out of the city.

"Where are we going?" asked Tariq.

His question was met with a hood being pulled over his head and instructions to shut up. Tariq was terrified, but he tried his best to show courage. This was most likely just standard operating procedure when dealing with powerful men who had huge bounties on their heads. The car jostled and whined as it worked its way out of the old section of the city to a highway. Tariq didn't know where he was, but when he felt the car hit smooth pavement and pick up speed, he knew he was on one of the major highways. Headed to *where*, he had no idea.

After an hour and a half of silence, one of the men up front instructed the man next to Tariq to remove the hood. Tariq blinked a few times and glanced around. He was on a major highway, which most likely meant Route 10. The highway cut through the orange desert like a road on Mars. As far as Tariq could see, there was nothing but wasteland and occasional steel towers from which hung heavy voltage wires. They allowed him to see, because there was nothing to be seen.

After another hour had passed, the men spoke in whispers up front, and the car slowed and made a right turn onto a smaller roadway. They snaked along a narrower two lane road, through rocky ravines and scrub grasses with herds of camels roaming freely through the desert. Tariq tried his best to get his bearings, knowing they had been heading east by the morning sun in his face. It had to be either Highway 10 or 40; they were the only major highways from Riyadh through the desert. Now that they had turned off, he was truly lost.

The car began bouncing again on squeaky shocks as the road became more primitive. As they came over a rise, a few farms with circular irrigation systems came into view—green circles on a Martian landscape. They drove off another road, and as they reached the area of irrigation, the wasteland came to life. Fields of crops appeared next to fields of solar panels. Barbed wire fences enclosed herds of cattle and sheep that roamed through fields of grass planted just for them. A large, well-maintained house appeared, and the car drove past it to another smaller house in the rear. They stopped, and Tariq and the others got out of the car.

There was no reason to speak. Tariq followed the men to the house, and they let themselves in. It was neat and comfortable inside, but they walked through the house and out the back door. Tariq found himself in the rear yard, which was enclosed by six foot stone walls. Dozens of sheep carcasses hung from a wire strung between two poles, the bloody sheepskins in a pile nearby. Alone at a small table sat Abu Mohamed, sipping tea under the shade of an awning.

He motioned for Tariq to sit with him, which he did. The men that had brought him stood silently nearby, out of the way.

Abu leaned forward and spoke quietly. "Fifty million dollars is quite a promise. What you asked for was also quite a large undertaking. I laid out millions to acquire your shipment. Millions of my own, as well as associates—investors, if you will. And now everyone needs to be paid. There was to be a truck."

"Of course. The truck was sent. The fifty million is yours," said Tariq nervously.

Abu leaned back and stroked the small chin beard. "The time and place was quite specific, Tariq. That was two days ago."

Tariq felt his mouth go dry. "The truck was sent. I don't understand?"

Abu looked over at his men, who immediately grabbed Tariq and had him up on his toes, one large man holding each arm very tightly. Abu walked over to the pile of sheep skins and picked up a long bloody knife.

He walked over to Tariq with the blade in his hands. "I'm only going to ask you one time. Where's the money?"

Tariq's face had turned white. "It was sent! Let me make a call!"

Abu studied him for a moment, and then spoke to his men. "Let him make his call."

Tariq pulled a cell phone from his pocket with a shaking hand. He had been given a number to call in case of emergency, but *only* in case of emergency. Tariq stared at the knife and dialed.

A gruff voice said, "Who is this?"

"It's Tariq. I came to pick up the shipment, but there's a problem."

A pause. "What problem?"

"The money. It never arrived."

"Of course it arrived! Don't let them double-cross us!"

"They say it didn't, and he has a knife," said Tariq, his voice trembling.

"I'll call you back in one minute," said the voice, which hung up before Tariq could protest.

Tariq relayed that back to Abu, who walked over to the skins and picked up a sharpening stone. He eyed Tariq and tossed the stone back in the dirt. "No, a dull blade will be better."

Tariq's eyes flooded with tears. He considered himself a brave Jihadist, prepared to die for Allah, but not like this. He had a mission to carry out.

An eternity went by, and the cell phone rang. Tariq answered.

A serious voice said, "The driver doesn't pick up."

"What do you mean?" stuttered Tariq.

"We'll get more money. Two days."

Tariq looked at Abu with pleading eyes. He managed to say, "Two days."

Abu Mohamed took the phone from Tariq's hand and spoke to the man on the other end. "You will call me about the money in two days. But you won't speak to Tariq. I want you to listen carefully now." He handed the phone to one of his men, and the two other men grabbed Tariq by the arms, holding him so tightly he couldn't move. The man with the phone held it towards Tariq and began shooting video. Abu grabbed Tariq's hair with one hand and began cutting his throat with the other. Tariq managed a long scream before he gurgled and blood squirted all over everyone. Abu kept cutting and sawing with the dull blade until he eventually severed Tariq's head. He dropped it on the ground and walked back to the table to pick up a cloth to wipe off his hands.

"Send the video to that number. Tell them *two days*, or I'll find every single one of them."

"What about him?" asked one of Abu's men.

"Bury it in the desert," sneered Abu Mohamed, and he walked back into the house.

CHAPTER 16

Palace of Prince Abdul bin-Mustafa Awadi

The prince was just back from racing in the desert. He had taken his 3.9 million dollar Lamborghini Veneno out for some fun. He had topped out at three hundred kilometers per hour and enjoyed quite a thrill. Now he was back at his palace, ready for a swim in one of his pools before his afternoon massage.

One of his assistants walked out of the house when he heard the Veneno roar up the circular driveway towards the fifty-car garage. He walked very quickly to the prince, his face showing his concern. The prince had enjoyed his morning, and he was angry before the man even spoke.

The assistant bowed slightly and showed Abdul a disposable cell phone. "There's been a serious problem," he said quietly. "The truck never arrived."

Abdul's face went pale. "What do you mean? That was two days ago. We're just hearing about this now?"

"The driver was told to deliver the truck and return home. He was only to call if there was an emergency. He never called, so it was assumed everything was fine. Just now, Tariq called. He was at the exchange."

"And?" asked Abdul.

"Abu Mohamed believed he had been double crossed. The money never arrived. He took it out on Tariq." He showed Abdul a picture on the cell phone from Tariq's number. It was Tariq's head on the ground near a pile of bloody sheep skins.

Abdul's mouth opened, but no sound came out. He finally managed to whisper a quiet prayer. "He was a loyal man," said Abdul. "Abu had no right."

"Fifty million dollars is missing. The package is out there somewhere. What do you want me to do? Abu Mohamed said he was giving us two days to replace the money, or he was going to come looking for all of us."

The prince looked at Tariq's head. He had a huge security detail, but he also didn't need any problems from the Islamist groups. "Get it done," was all he managed to say as he walked away.

CHAPTER 17

CIA Training Facility

The team had started their morning in a small classroom, with Kim Elton teaching Middle Eastern politics. She was a bright lady and had the ability to take something extremely complicated and "dumb it down" so that a room full of jarheads, SEALs, and rangers could understand it. A two-hour lesson on who was trying to kill whom, who was in power with what organization, and which organization was operating where, went very quickly.

When the team was mentally fried, it was time for some physical ass-whooping. They were dismissed, and an instructor led them to a mulched path in the woods behind the building.

"I usually run the training exercises here. Quite frankly, you don't need me. Follow the trail for a mile. Once you get to the confidence course, I'm sure you'll know what to do. Have fun." He turned and walked away.

Cascaes barked at Moose. "You heard the man. Turn this Little League parade into a column of twos that resembles a fighting force!"

Moose smiled and happily began screaming. "The only easy day was yesterday, ladies! Column of twos and everyone stays tight. Move!"

The men shuffled around and magically transformed from a group of men standing near each other, to a platoon of Special Forces in perfect order. As soon as they were in a tight column of twos, with the two Chrises in the back and Moose alongside like the Drill Instructor, Moose yelled "double time!" and they began running the trail. Five and a half minutes later, they were a mile down the path staring at a confidence course similar to the one affectionately known as "The Yellow Brick Road" in Quantico used by the Marines and FBI.

"Six miles of fun, ladies. Get busy!" barked Moose as he increased his speed down the hill towards the course. The six miles included a ten foot wall to scale, which was only accomplished by team work, several tiny foot bridges and poles to move across, a series of rope ladders and, of course, the three story tower to climb and rope over. For Marine recruits, it would be considered a challenging confidence builder—for these special operators, it was like being allowed out to the playground after class. They pushed themselves and each other, climbing, roping, running, and screaming at each other. Mackey and Cascaes went through just like everyone else, and even though Mackey was clearly a step behind, the fact that he could handle the course at his age was nothing but inspirational to everyone else.

After crawling under rope obstacles, climbing over mounted poles and bars and sprinting through the mud, the team reached the three story tower. Eric Hodges, the team Marine sniper, and Earl Jones, another Marine Recondo, were the first two to reach the base of the tower.

"I fucking hate the tower, man," whispered Earl as he grabbed the bottom rung and hoisted himself up.

"Don't like heights?" asked Eric, pulling and climbing alongside him.

"No. I hated this shit at Parris Island, and I hate it now."

Eric laughed. "Snipers are always looking for a tower to climb. Just keep looking up!"

Earl grunted and climbed, moving with tremendous speed and agility. "I didn't say I don't know *how* to do it, I said I don't *like* it!"

The two of them led the others straight up the tower without stopping. It wasn't until they got to the top and had to throw their legs over that Earl's face showed his apprehension. Eric patted Earl on the back, threw his own leg over, and grabbed one of the ropes he'd be using to work his way down. He handed a section of rope towards Earl and said, "Keep moving, Marine!"

Earl grabbed the rope, looked up and mumbled some obscenity, and threw himself over the top. They began climbing down, section by section, passing their team ascending on the other side. Moose never shut up the entire climb, pushing the team to move faster. By the time everyone was over and they were reassembled at the base, they were all soaked with sweat. Mackey was huffing and puffing, and managed to cough out his usual, "I'm getting too old for this shit..."

Moose had everyone back in formation, screaming to "finish strong" and the group ran all the way back to the beginning of the course. There was no way for them to know they had just set a new course record.

Once back at the main building, the men showered and changed clothes, then ate lunch and took a bus to the shooting range located about a mile from the building in the middle of the property.

At the range the men assembled weapons and set up targets. Eric Hodges spent extra time assembling his new toy, a prototype sniper rifle known as a PSR. The Precision Sniper Rifle had been issued to Special Forces snipers over a year ago as the replacement sniper rifle for American forces.

While the other men blasted away at targets, relentlessly hitting bulls-eyes, Hodges took his time assembling and admiring his Remington. As he began snapping the large rounds into the clips, Moose walked over.

"New toy fires mortar rounds?" he asked, eyeing the large shells.

"Lapua .338s," he replied in his heavy Oklahoma drawl.

"Lapua. Why does that sound familiar?" asked Moose.

"Higher velocity at long range. These are what that British sniper was using in Afghanistan when he set the record for longest confirmed kill. 2,475 meters. That's a little over 2700 yards."

"Jesus. Yeah, I think I remember that. He must have fired the round on Monday and hit the guy on Wednesday."

Hodges smiled. "Muzzle velocity is 3,000 feet per second. I'm guessing the Taliban dude had enough time to hear the shot and say, '*What was that?*'"

"Snipers. Sit around all day waiting for one shot," mumbled Moose. "Give me a belt-fed weapon any day."

"Spray and pray, Moose? Nah. I'll wait all day and fire one round. And you can be damn sure I'll hit what I aim at." He glanced around. "Shame about those kids, though." He clucked his tongue and spit. Eric had seen the windshield explode when he killed the driver of the truck. He didn't have enough time to see that the other occupants were children, but it wouldn't have mattered anyway—Cascaes was in danger, and he had acquired a target with an AK47 at the ready.

Moose nodded but didn't say anything. He wasn't there at the ambush, but he knew what had gone down. Eric snapped the five-round magazine into his rifle and hoisted it on his back along with his field pack, and then began walking further away from the range. Moose looked back at the target, which was barely visible in front of a large earthen berm.

He shook his head and decided to follow Hodges. They walked for five minutes before Eric stopped and dropped his pack gently on the ground. Moose could see the large berm off in the distance, but not the target.

Eric opened his pack and rummaged to find a box with a spotter scope in it. He handed it to Moose. "Earl's busy trying to learn to shoot straight. You can play spotter."

Eric knelt down and pulled his rifle from his shoulder, then pulled the covers off his scope. He laid down on his stomach and made himself comfortable. Moose laid down next to him

and opened the small tripod on the spotter scope, then looked
through it.

"Wow. These are powerful."

"You mean to tell me you never looked through a spotter
before?"

"Why would I?" asked Moose.

Eric shrugged. "I figured everyone in the world wanted to
be a sniper or a spotter. Don't worry about wind speed or range.
I'll do everything. Just look through and watch the vapor trail
after I fire. You should see the round impact the target."

"How far is that?" asked Moose.

"Range is 1,800 meters. Or, if you want, I can hit Ripper
from here. He's only about 1,500 and a much bigger target."

"Leave my catcher alone. Now let me see you hit that thing.
I can barely see it even with this thing."

Eric pushed ear plugs into his ears, and Moose did the same.
He adjusted his scope for a few seconds and then quietly said
to Moose, "Heading downrange."

The sound was louder than Moose anticipated, and he was
even more surprised when he was able to see the round's vapor
trail before impact. Eric hit the target dead center. He repeated
the shot four more times, about ten seconds apart, each round
within an inch of the preceding round.

"Jesus," whispered Moose.

Eric placed the covers back on his scope. "Dad was a Marine
and Grandpa was a Marine. Gramps was a sniper in the South
Pacific during World War Two. He had me shooting squirrels
and gophers by the time I was five. I grew up in the middle of
nowhere. Keeping varmints off the crops was a daily chore.
Gramps always said a sniper needs patience, steady hands, and
a good rifle. This here rifle is a game changer."

Moose was standing, squinting at the berm. "And some
God-given talent. No one else on the team would have made
that shot, Eric."

Eric started walking out even farther.

"Where are you going now?" asked Moose.

"2,500."

"You shitting me?" asked Moose.

"Don't worry about the mule, you just load the wagon," replied Hodges, quoting two generations of Hodges men.

CHAPTER 18

The team trained hard all day. When they were finished for the day, they returned to the housing facility to shower and change. Normally, when agents were training at the facility, they lived there twenty-four-seven until the course was finished. The team made its own rules, however, and Mackey called Dex and told him he was taking the boys out for pizza and beer.

Dex didn't love the idea of the men being out and about together at first, but then decided if they were a Navy All-Star Team, it wouldn't be unusual for them to have pizza and beer together. He authorized it and arranged for a bus to drive them to DC.

Mackey's announcement to the team that they were headed to Angelino's Pizza in DC was met with a huge ovation. When Cascaes announced he was buying the first round, the ovation continued for another full minute.

An hour later, the team was on board a black bus headed to DC. The bus stopped near a parking lot and unloaded the team, and the sixteen hungry men entered the crowded pizza joint. A table for sixteen was going to take a while, so the men made their way to the bar and began ordering pitchers of beer. There were pool tables in the back, and once they had beers in hand, most of the men headed back to play pool and drink some beer while they waited. Mackey and Cascaes sat on two bar stools at the end of the bar and smiled at the sight of their men acting like college kids.

"We've got a good crew," said Mackey as he watched Ripper and Moose laughing and back slapping each other. Chris nodded.

"You don't say a whole hellova lot, do ya?" asked Mackey. "I've known you for years and I still don't *know* you."

Chris made a surprised face. "Guess I've never been big on small talk."

Mackey got him another beer. "I'll get you drunk and get your life story."

Chris took a long drink. "You want my life story? It ain't all that, trust me."

"I do trust you. And you should trust me, too. So give me something. Where'd you grow up? How did you end up in the Navy?"

Chris took a deep breath. Talking about himself was out of his comfort zone, but Mackey had become one of his trusted friends—in fact, one of his only friends. "Okay. I'll give you the life story. Then we don't talk about it again, okay?"

Mackey extended his hand. "Deal."

They shook hands firmly.

"I grew up in Newark, New Jersey in the Iron Bound. Portuguese neighborhood. My father Ray was a first class drunken prick. Apparently he was nice to my mother at least once, because they had me. Then he decided my mom made a better punching bag than wife, and I watched him beat the crap out of her a few times a week for most of my first fourteen years on the planet. He popped me a few times, too, but Mom always got it worse. Eventually, I got old enough to know he was a psycho that needed a good ass kicking. I was just too small, so I started reading about martial arts. Eventually started hanging out at this Karate studio, watching this Japanese sensei teach his classes. I guess a few months of me stalking the place eventually went noticed, along with the occasional black eyes, and the old man started talking to me, asking me questions about why I was always there. I told him I wanted to learn karate, but I didn't have any money. He asked me if I was having a problem at school because I had a pretty good shiner that day. I told him it wasn't school, and he figured it out for himself. Invited me to attend his school if I'd clean up and work for him doing whatever he needed doing. My parents never knew where I was anyway, so I started going there every day."

"I can see where this is going," said Mackey quietly.

"Yup." Chris took a long drink from his beer, draining his glass. Mackey refilled it immediately. "So I studied hard and this Master, Kenji Mokai , took me under his wing. Within a year, I became a pretty lethal weapon." He took another long drink. "So one night, I'm home and Ray comes home blasted out of his skull and wants dinner. Mom had worked late that night and dinner wasn't ready. Ray started beating the shit out of her, as usual."

"Was Ray your real dad?" asked Mackey. "I mean, you call him Ray."

"I call him Ray because that piece of shit doesn't deserve to be called dad. So anyway, he was beating her up pretty good and I'd had enough. I walked over and roundhouse kicked him as hard as I could in the solar plexus, just as I'd practiced for a year. Dropped him like a rock and told him he was never laying a finger on either of us ever again. When he tried to get up I broke his jaw and laid him out. My mother was begging me to leave before he woke up."

"Jeez," mumbled Mackey.

"I told her the only one that was leaving was him. He didn't wake up until the next morning. He remembered what happened and tried to get in my face, but I put him in a wrist lock and bounced his face off the floor, broken jaw and all. Put my knee in his back and told him if he ever touched my mom or me again, I'd kill him. Then I smashed his face a few times against the floor to make sure he knew I was serious. He stumbled out of the house and that was the last I saw of him.

Some weeks later, he came back during the day and took a bunch of stuff from the house and left a nasty note for Mom. I found it before she got home and ditched it.

"A few years later, right when I graduated high school, Mom decided to get hammered and drive home late. Wrapped herself around a pole."

"Jesus, Chris, I'm sorry," said Mackey.

Chris shrugged and finished his beer again, which Mackey refilled. "So, with no parents and no money, I decided to see the world. Joined the Navy and never looked back. I have to say, it was the best thing I ever did. First time I was ever really happy I think." He paused and reflected for a moment. "Man, the first time I was aboard a ship…" He looked Mackey in the eyes. "Greatest day of my life."

Mackey hoisted his glass and toasted him.

"Anyway, I took every class, every course, every assignment. Decided I was a lifer. Ended up making the SEALs, and the rest is history. And now that you know that shitty-ass story, you don't ever have to ask me again."

Mackey nodded. "Yeah, you're a barrel of laughs. Let's get some pizza and drink beers until I forget everything you just told me."

CHAPTER 19

Mackey stood up, but Chris gently grabbed his arm. "Whoa," he exclaimed.

Mackey looked at him, surprised.

"I just told you more about me than I've told anyone in twenty years. Your turn, sit down."

Mackey stared at him, then sat. He rubbed his chin. "I like interrogations to go the other way."

"Exactly," said Chris. He poured a beer and slid it to Mackey. "Your turn, Mack. Spill it."

Mackey looked at the beer and made a face. "Okay, fine. Fair's fair." He took a long drink and sat with his back against the bar, watching his team playing pool and laughing. "Good bunch of guys."

"Nice try. Spill it."

Mackey rubbed his chin again. "I grew up in God's country. Iowa. Not to rub it in, but I was lucky with my family. My folks were great. Hard working, simple folks who ran a big farm. Dad is Chris, *senior*, so I grew up as Mack. I grew up working the farm with my brother Wyatt. He's three years younger than me. The real farmer of the family.

"Dad had lived on the same farm all his life. My grandparents' farm. He was a pilot flying crop dusters when the Japanese bombed Pearl Harbor. Dad enlisted in the air force the next day. Because he was already a pilot, they grabbed him up and had him flying fighters in the Pacific as fast as they could get him there. When he came home, he went back to farming and flying crop dusters for most of the farms in our area. I think he made more money flying than farming. I was born in '53. Learned to drive the family pickup at ten, but I was learning to fly when I was younger. I sat copilot every time dad went up. I loved flying as much as he did, and he could see that in me. He loved to fly, too, and I think it was good therapy. When I got older and flew in Vietnam, we traded war stories. First time he ever talked about his years in the Pacific we both had a good cry. They lost *so* many guys back in those days.

"Anyway, Dad and I had a great relationship and he had me flying for real by the time I was fifteen. He turned over the crop dusting business to me, and I built it up to a decent little business." He laughed.

Chris looked at him. "That's funny?"

"No, just thinking back. When I would finish dusting, I'd find a field where no one was around and do aerobatics and crazy shit the plane wasn't designed for. It's a wonder I never crashed that old bird, but it made me a good flyer. Loved those days.

"When I turned eighteen, it was 1975 and the war was still going on. Dad's World War Two pictures had been on the wall for my whole life. He was the coolest, man. Like the old movie stars in the black and white movies. The day after my birthday, I told Dad I was enlisting in the air force. Dad figured I'd get drafted anyway. Better to be above the jungle than in it, so off I went. I was already a good pilot, and they put me in an OV-10 Bronco. It was a prop plane not much bigger than my crop duster, except it was a wicked good fighter surveillance plane."

"So were you taking pictures or doing fire missions?" asked Chris.

Mackey sighed. "Well, recon missions had a way of turning into fire missions. I'd go out to gather intel and take pictures, and invariably, some ground troops would hit the radio screaming for help, and off I'd go. The Broncos weren't really

thought of as close ground support, but they could be very
effective. I'd get close, act as forward air controller, and guide
in the fast movers."

"Any close calls?"

Mack studied Chris a moment. "This is between us."

"Sure," said Chris quietly, now fully curious.

"I had over a hundred combat missions. Only one of them
was what I'd really call close." He took a long drink of his beer
and scanned around to make sure they had some privacy. "I was
up doing what I did every day. Looking for SAM sites, troop
movements, the usual shit. I get a call from ground troops, and
I could hear it in the radioman's voice, you know? The kid
was terrified. I think he was crying. I could hear small arms
fire in the background. They were being overrun. I got him
to calm down and give me his location, then hauled ass over
there and started strafing the dinks. Sorry—Vietnamese. Our
guys were in a rice paddy in a trap. Mine field had them pinned
and they were getting shredded by the NVA in the jungle all
around them. I flew circle after circle, firing everything I had.
Machine guns, rockets." He sipped his beer, his eyes looking
into his past.

"Small arms fire began taking my Bronco apart. I got hit
a few times in the legs and forearm. My plane had a little
fire cooking in the cockpit. But that kid on the ground kept
directing fire, and I could see how close the enemy was.
Mortars and RPGs pounding our guys. I couldn't leave—no
way. So I just kept at it. I finally managed to get some close air
support called in, and the jets naped the jungle and ended the
fight. By the time I got back to base, my plane and I were both
in pretty rough shape."

"Shit," said Chris quietly. "Purple Heart for that one?"

Mackey flashed a fake smile. "And a Silver Star. The
sergeant on the ground insisted on finding out who saved their
ass and was relentless about that medal. We actually stayed

good friends for years after the war. He died a few years ago; Agent Orange most likely."

Chris clinked his glass. "To the fearless flyer."

Mack clinked his glass, but said, "I was too busy to be scared at first, but let me tell you, the flight back to base, bleeding all over, watching the plane burn—I thought I was toast, man. Scared shitless.

"So anyway, I did two tours and then one day a guy in a suit shows up."

"CIA?" asked Chris.

"If I tell you, I'll have to kill you. Yeah. The company. They pulled me from the air force and a few months later I was flying in Russian, Chinese, and Korean airspace on a regular basis. Not that I ever said that, or you ever heard it. I ended up liking what I was doing. It was exciting. And I wasn't in East Bumblefuck, Iowa, anymore. I told my dad what I was doing, but as far as Mom and Wyatt knew, I was flying commercial jets and was away a lot. I always managed a few trips a year home to visit. Thanksgiving every year for sure. Mom and Dad are both gone now, and Wyatt runs the farm with his wife and three boys. We keep in touch."

Chris nodded, thinking how nice it must have been to have a normal family. He pictured a white picket fence and a farmhouse, then his crazy drunk father, and took a swig. "Ever married?"

Mack laughed. "No. For the same reasons as you. How the hell do you have a normal relationship with anyone when you can't tell her what you do, and you're never fucking home?"

Chris smiled. "Yup."

"Got laid plenty, though." They clinked glasses and laughed. "When I was running a few things with the Russians, I had a few chicks inside that I used to use for information, you know? Man, those Russian chicks were so friggin' hot. I swear I was ready to go KGB after a weekend with this one Ukrainian chick." He laughed and closed his eyes for a second, picturing the most beautiful woman he'd ever seen.

"Anyway, by the time I was forty, I knew I was a bachelor for life. I'm way too fucked up now to be a good husband."

Chris laughed. "Yeah, I hear you. I think about the shit I've done and seen. How could I ever have a normal conversation with anybody about anything?"

"Exactly. My few friends are guys like you. The guys I trust with my life that I work with. That's about it. And the occasional piece of ass for a very short interval, until they ask me questions I can't answer." He shrugged. "In my next life I'll fly for United and have six kids."

"Yeah, right," said Chris with a laugh. He looked over at the group of guys drinking and laughing by the pool table. They'd kill and die for him and vice-versa. *They* were his family. He thought about what Dex had said earlier. Some guy named Hill wanted him out—wanted the team to fail. The thought of his family being taken apart and dispersed out into the armed forces made him angry. They wouldn't fail. His men would never let him down, and he'd die before he'd fail them.

Mack laughed, too. "Well, in *this* life, I'm going to retire and buy a big boat down south somewhere. I'll be drinking cold beer and fishing and chasing pretty girls. You can come visit when you're on R and R."

"Deal," said Chris.

A young waitress walked over to them and told them that their table had been set up. It was time for pizza.

CHAPTER 20

CIA Training Facility

The team had stayed out until the place closed, eating more pizza and drinking more beer than the rest of the patrons combined. It had been a much-needed night off, and the men had blown off steam and had a chance to socialize in a different type of setting. They had felt human again.

Cascaes was up at oh-five thirty, walking the hallway like a Marine Drill Instructor with a baseball bat banging against a metal trash can. "Wake up, ladies!" he screamed as he walked up and down the hall.

The men had years of mental conditioning, and they rolled out of their beds, hung-over and exhausted, but with a reflex to be outside and standing at semi-formal attention in the hallway in their boxers. Moose was his typical self, screaming at his SEALs to move faster. Once they were assembled, they looked at Chris, puzzled at the boot camp awakening.

"I can't have you getting soft, you fat bodies!" yelled Chris. "Mess hall in fifteen, outside to the trail in thirty! Move it, people!"

The men ran back inside to hop into shorts and shirts, and Mackey walked out of his room, moving much slower than everyone else. "You shittin' me?" he asked Cascaes.

"You're excused from duty on account of being very fucking old. These guys need an ass-kicking," he said calmly.

81

"See you at breakfast." With that, he put down the garbage can and walked towards the mess hall.

The team ate quietly and quickly, not overeating for two reasons, they were still full from pizza night, and they didn't want to throw up all over themselves. Cascaes' SEALs knew what an early morning wakeup call meant, and it was never good.

Chris had them outside, column of twos fifteen minutes later, and was surprised to see Mackey outside with them. Chris made eye contact, and Mackey flipped him the bird. Chris jogged to the front of the column, and then took off.

"The only easy day was yesterday!" he bellowed as he ran down the trail. The men took off after him at a faster pace than usual. It was going to be one of those kind of days.

At two o'clock, the team jogged back to where they started, thoroughly soaked with sweat through their clothes on a cold, wet afternoon. Five of them had thrown up off to the side of the trail at various times, and they had all sweated out the alcohol from the night before. It had been their hardest workout in weeks, but the truth was, they all loved it. They were simply a different breed of human.

Once back at the main building, Chris dismissed the men to shower up and meet for a late lunch at three. They had taken water breaks, but hadn't eaten since their light breakfast before the sun had come up.

Chris and Mackey stood outside and watched the men head inside to shower and change. Once the men were out of sight, Mack stepped into the bushes and puked. After spitting a few times, he walked back over to Chris and shook his head. "You're right. I'm way too fucking old for this shit."

"You hung right in there and you weren't the only one puking. Quit your bitching. You would have made a good SEAL a few years back."

"I liked sitting in the plane."

"You never did tell me, did you get your pecker shot off that day?" asked Chris with his usual slight grin. The man wasn't big on belly laughing.

"Happy to say I have all my original parts. But don't laugh. I used to sit on a piece of steel plate for that exact reason. We have a briefing in thirty minutes with Dex and Kim."

"Roger that. See you there."

⊕

Thirty minutes later, the two Chrises arrived at Dex's office, where Kim was already seated.

"To what do I owe the pleasure?" asked Mack.

"More chatter," he replied. "Kim…"

Kim asked the men to sit, which they did. Dex was behind his desk, Kim in a high backed chair, and Mack and Chris on a leather coach.

"We don't have a lot of assets that we trust in Qatar, which has been limiting. Oman and the UAE have limited help, and they aren't hearing anything. We do have some field presence in Saudi, but it's a tough place to work. The Mabahith, that's the Saudi Secret Police, they keep a close eye on our folks. They know who our people are most of the time, and we're very careful about pissing off our Saudi allies."

"So what's the chatter?" asked Mack, not following her conversation.

"Saudi contacts in a bank watched another fifty million leave Prince Abdul Awadi's account again."

"We're wired into their bank?" asked Chris.

"No, unfortunately, their anti-terrorism laws are almost as bad as Qatar's, and we aren't allowed access to their banking information."

"So…?" asked Mack.

"So we do have a few low level bank employees on our payroll. They do a little snooping for us into specific account balances. It's how we caught the fifty million this morning. It was a cash transaction."

"Fifty million in cash and no one asks any questions?" asked Chris.

"Nope. Welcome to the Middle East. Awadi buys a racing car every few months for cash, too. A few hundred thousand dollars in a duffle bag. An everyday occurrence out there in oil land."

"I bought a truck for cash once," said Chris quietly. "Back in Iowa. It was five hundred bucks."

"So we think this is the replacement fifty million for the fifty we *acquisitioned* last week?" asked Mack.

"Precisely. We can't prove anything, of course. But we're going to arrange a rematch with the prince's baseball team. We need you to get inside his palace. Our tech guys have been working on a few new gadgets. If you can get into the palace and get to a computer—any computer inside the palace, we can get into his entire network," said Kim.

"Sure wouldn't mind the rematch," said Mackey. "I had to throw the last game and it's been pissing me off every day since."

"He's funny that way," said Cascaes. "Thinks he's really coaching a baseball team."

"So you didn't mind losing?" asked Kim, smiling.

"I didn't lose with those half-assed baseball players. I was out stealing fifty million dollars." He almost smirked.

Dex chuckled. "Then it's settled. You're going back to Eskan and playing baseball. Get inside the palace, bug the shit out of his computers and phones, and we'll get ourselves some proof and gather some information."

"Phones?" asked Mack. "I thought it was a computer thing?"

Kim smiled. "We'll take you to the barn. It's what we call the tech building. They have a tiny little gadget that just needs to be inside the palace to get into the prince's Wi-Fi network and every satellite communication in and out. Between listening to his phone calls and reading his emails, we should be able to nail his ass."

Mack looked at Chris and in his best umpire voice said, *"Play ball!"*

CHAPTER 21

Mackey was sitting in the dugout watching his team stretch and get warmed up. Moose was throwing to Ripper in the bullpen while Ernie warmed up with Jon a few feet away. Moose could throw a fastball like any major league pro, while Ernie relied on breaking balls. Jake Koches had been stretching and jogging in the outfield when he stopped and then ran across the field to the other team. Mackey watched curiously for a while as Jake and some player on the prince's team chatted and laughed together. They shook hands and Jake jogged back towards his team. Mackey whistled at him to grab his attention and called him to the dugout.

"What was that all about? Who's he?" asked Mackey.

Jake looked at him and smiled. "You don't recognize him? That A-rab did it again. Hired pros. That's Mike Duffy! He played for the Mets for ten years, Mack! Retired last year, but the prince offered him a hundred and fifty grand *cash* to fly out here first class and play baseball for a few days. He's not as good as he used to be, but he's a hell of a lot better than any of *us*!"

Mack folded his arms on his chest. "They had pros last time, too, and we almost beat them. I don't want to hear that shit. What position does he play?"

"Third base. But he's got a serious bat, Mack. He'll be knocking them over the fence all day, no offense to Moose or Ernie. They better walk his ass."

"So noted. Anyone else over there you recognize?"

86

"Duffy is the only one I recognized right away, but Mike told me there's four other American pros on the team. They've been here for three days living like kings. Well, like princes, anyway." He laughed at his own joke.

"This prince is pissing me off. I know winning the game isn't why we're here, but I'm a sore loser—and unless you and your friends want to be PTed[2] to *death*, you better play like you want to win."

Jake's smile disappeared. "Yes, sir," was all he replied, and he jogged back out to the field to continue loosening up.

Mackey kicked the dirt and checked his watch. Almost game time. Music came on, and Mackey looked up to see the prince walking down the steps behind home plate with his entourage. There were over a dozen of his friends, all dressed in formal thobes, long white robes, with kuffiyehs of either red and white or black and white on their heads. A few pairs of high-end French sunglasses were thrown in for good measure.

Mackey stared at them as they made their way down, waving to players who waved back. The prince gave a "papal wave" to Mackey, who returned it with his best Queen Elizabeth impersonation, the sarcasm lost on the prince.

Mackey's team jogged back into the dugout and Mackey read off the batting order. As soon as he was finished with that, he gave a quick pep talk to his team.

"I hate this fucker. Go out there and win a baseball game. Moose, don't give number five anything to swing at; Jakes says he's some Duffy guy from the Mets. I gotta talk to Langley and get a bigger budget for this op. We need a few pros on our team. In the meantime, try not to screw this up. Eric, get on base—that's an order."

The two teams lined up along the baselines for the formality of the National Anthem, followed by the Saudi Anthem, and then returned to their dugouts. Eric walked to home plate and

---

[2] Physical training

tapped his cleats with his bat, which had been corked back at Langley by their "gadgets folks." If the prince could bring in ringers, the team could cheat, too.

Cascaes walked out to first base, on the pretext of being the first base coach. He aimed his baseball hat at the prince and his associates and casually squeezed the bill of the cap, turning on the powerful camera hidden in the cap. He slowly scanned every face around the prince, which was being seen in real-time back at Langley by facial recognition systems as well as Middle East analysts and Kim Elton. If any of the prince's guests were in the system, they'd know soon enough.

Eric took the first two pitches, a ball and a strike, and then looked back at Mackey, who didn't signal. Eric was free to do what he wanted. He watched another fastball come in at ninety miles an hour, strike two. The next pitch was also a fastball, but hit the outside corner where Eric made contact. The corked center made the ball take off like a Fungo bat, and the ball bounced off the top of the center field wall.

Ripper, who was batting second, grabbed the bat and tossed it back towards the dugout before their catcher could grab it to inspect it. Anyone who knew baseball would have been a little suspicious of how lively that hit was, but no one said anything. Ripper stood at the plate, a giant of a man, with his bat looking like a toothpick in his hands. The pitcher threw him some chin music to set the tone, but Ripper never backed off the plate. Ripper merely stared at the pitcher and pointed his bat, like he was aiming straight at him. The two of them stared at each other, and the next pitch was a breaking ball for ball two. A swing and a miss, another ball, a called strike, and then *wham!* A line drive right back at the pitcher made the pitcher cover up for a near miss. It went through the middle for a single that moved Eric to third base. Ripper and the pitcher stared at each other for a second as he stood on first base smiling. Ripper wasn't actually good enough to aim right at the pitcher, but the way things turned out sure made him happy. His teammates in the dugout cheered wildly, just to piss the pitcher off.

Raul was batting third, and his groundball led to a double play, but Eric managed to score their first run. Lance was batting cleanup and managed to tease everyone with a shot to the wall, but it was caught with a sensational play from the professional centerfielder.

The team took the field with confidence and poise and proceeded to get shelled for ten minutes with the score at the end of one, four to one. Moose was throwing hard—the problem was these guys were just damn good.

For baseball fans that weren't into pitching duels, it was a fun game to watch, with the lead changing twice by the time they got to the ninth inning. At the bottom of the ninth, the prince's team had tied the game, and they went into extra innings.

Mackey welcomed his players back into the dugout for the top of the tenth. "I know my team isn't tired. My team is the most bad-ass assemblage of war lords on the motherfucking planet. Look over at their dugout! A bunch of retirees who need oxygen. No one needs to hit a homer. Just make them keep running around. They're tired and they don't give a shit if they win—they're getting paid either way. You *do* give a shit if you win, because if you lose I will have you running and working out until you die. Now get out there and hit the ball. And cheat if you have to!"

It was bottom of the order, and Moose was up. He looked at his normal bat, and then decided on the corked one instead. He looked at Eric and whispered, "You stay in the on-deck circle and grab this friggin' bat if it breaks."

"Roger that. Send it downrange," said Eric quietly.

Moose walked out to the plate and looked at the other pitcher. They had replaced their starter in the seventh inning, and Moose had switched places with Ernie P. in the eighth.

Moose had thrown a lot of pitches, but he was a beast, and was fresh and itching to swing.

After watching the first two, Moose made contact with the third pitch and sent it so far it bounced off the scoreboard four hundred feet away. He threw the bat to Eric, who jogged it back to the dugout. The American catcher, retired from the Twins, stood up and pulled his mask off. He turned to the umpire and screamed "Bullshit!" as Moose rounded second. While the catcher complained to the umpire, Eric and his teammates switched bats, which they then produced for the umpire, who inspected it, tapped it, hefted it, and examined it again for several minutes. He was still holding it when Moose crossed home plate and demanded to know what they were doing.

The umpire declared the bat was legal, to which Moose agreed. "Of course it is! It's not my fault if I hit it out of the dome." He smiled and jogged back to the dugout where his teammates snickered and avoided eye contact.

Eric was now up, and couldn't use the loaded bat with everyone now watching. Instead, he laid down a bunt and sprinted like a fresh track star to first, beating the throw. The other team was showing their fatigue and frustration, and the prince called the coach, demanding a pitching change. The coach reluctantly put in the third pitcher, who was an Arab, and not a professional. And while it wasn't what he wanted to do strategically, he wasn't going to ever say no to the sheikh.

The new pitcher took the mound and warmed up. He looked terrified. The Navy All Stars stood in the dugout watching him warm up and licked their lips.

Ripper walked to the plate. The pitcher's first batter was the largest man he'd seen in years with arms that barely fit in his shirt sleeves. The pitcher kicked the dirt, played with his hat, and talked to himself. He threw the first pitch, which literally bounced in front of the plate, the catcher making a good stop. The catcher, another American ringer, yelled encouragement in English. The second pitch hit Ripper in the upper arm, and Ripper took a step towards him. He stared at the terrified kid a moment, then dropped the bat and jogged to first. Mackey took great pleasure watching the prince's face up in the stands. The man was a nice shade of purple.

Raul was up next, and the poor kid on the mound aimed a pitch instead of throwing it. It hung over the plate and Raul crushed it to the left field alley. A stand up double had Ripper crossing home plate. The go-ahead run. From there, the wheels came off the bus. The catcher twice asked to inspect the bat, but chose two times when they were legitimate bats. When two men were on base and Jon Cohen got to the plate, he grabbed another cork special and put it over the wall for a three-run homer. Mackey was praying the umpire's hearing wasn't as good as his. The ball definitely sounded funny coming off the bat, but Raul had grabbed the bat and thrown it into the dugout before it could be inspected. By the time the home team was back up, the score was eleven to seven.

Ernie P. was fresh and feeling good. While he didn't have Moose's power, his curves and sliders were good stuff, and with only one single, they retired the side and won the game. The prince was obviously outraged, after paying huge sums of money to import ringers to win the game, but he was obliged to once again offer a feast to his guests. This time, Mackey happily accepted, and his team hit the showers.

CHAPTER 22

The Navy All Stars enjoyed hot showers in the prince's locker room. It was nicer than most resorts in the world, and the men took their time with fancy soap and shampoo, steam showers and whirlpool baths.

Bathroom attendants brought them lemon water and fruit platters to enjoy as they changed into their team sweat suits. Ninety minutes later, the fresh-looking crew followed Mackey to the bus, which brought them back to the prince's palace located only a mile away. The team bus rumbled along a quarter-mile long private cobblestone driveway, lined with palm trees and statues. The men were in awe when the bus pulled up in front of the palace. It was surreal in its opulence, with architecture that was a cross between Arab mosque and Baroque, with endless statues and fountains.

The team was received outside the palace by a long line of servants and one of the prince's wives. They were then escorted through a long marble hallway that was as fine in accoutrements as any five-star hotel or art museum. The men looked around in silent amazement at the paintings, statues, chandeliers, and furniture. The marble for the walls and floors had been imported from Italy and Africa and masterfully put together to from intricate designs. The grand ballroom, where they would be dining, was big enough to accommodate a hundred dinner guests at one long table. The table itself was mahogany with mother of pearl inlay and solid gold legs that had been hand engraved and adorned with gemstones. Everywhere the men looked, they stared in amazement.

Ernie P. and Smitty were now about to get to work. Each of them had multiple electronic listening devices in hidden pockets all over their clothes. The small devices had been designed by Langley's techs to intercept wireless communications including all Wi-Fi, phone, and satellite communications that would occur inside the palace once they were operating. The only downside to these high-tech toys was that they needed to be inside the network they were bugging. It was for this reason only that they had asked for a rematch and planned on being in the palace after the game.

"Dude's table is bigger than the apartment building where I grew up," whispered Earl to Raul.

"Yeah, man, no shit. Probably more expensive, too. I was in a few palaces in Iraq during the war, but they were blown up and looted already. This shit's off the hook, bro," said Raul.

The three hours that followed were course after course of amazing gourmet food. It was mostly French food, with some local Middle Eastern favorites mixed in as well. The men ate like they were going to the electric chair. As they awaited dessert, Smitty asked a waiter where the men's room was. As he walked out of the dining room, he stopped at the prince's chair at the head of the table.

"Excuse me, your eminence, but I was wondering, do you have a computer somewhere that I could use? I'd love to check in at home with a quick email. We just had a baby, and I'm missing my new son," lied Smitty.

"You are Joe Smith, the infielder. You played very well today," said the prince. "Of course, you may help yourself to a computer." The prince snapped his fingers, and a servant quickly came to his side. The prince said a few words in Arabic, and the man motioned for Joe to follow him.

Smitty walked a long hallway to another room, were there was an ornate antique desk of carved and inlaid wood that cost more than Smitty's apartment. The man pointed to a computer desktop and walked over, waking up the hibernating machine and keying in the password. He then opened a drawer and pulled out another keyboard, this one in English, and turned it on after he turned the first one off. The machine found the new keyboard, and they were all set. In broken English, the servant said, "I wait," and walked outside the doorway.

Smitty slid a small sticky device, no bigger than a sunflower seed out of a plastic packet in his pocket. Figuring he was on close circuit TV, Smitty concealed his movement. He leaned forward like he was staring at the screen and reached under the desk above his knees. He moved his fingers around until he found a tiny opening were he pushed the device. He then quickly checked over his shoulder and made sure the servant was still outside. He began typing into a false email account that looked innocent enough with the name *mrsrachaelsmith*, and he opened up the email that had been left for him by the Langley techs. By opening the mail, he released a program into the machine that would be undetectable to any virus software. The program would infiltrate every computer on the network and would turn this machine into a wireless hunter that would also find every other machine within the palace and pull its data. The small seed in the desk would bug every phone and dish antennae. To keep up appearances, Smitty sat back and looked lovingly at a baby picture. He typed in big letters, "I love you and miss you both so much," then sent the email. He closed up the server and left, thanking the servant and returning to dinner.

⊕

"I love you, too, Smitty," said Kim Elton to her computer screen in Langley. She watched a tree open up on her screen that began showing computer after computer popping up on the prince's network. Twenty-two machines, some of which were backup drives, were now wide open for review. Kim grabbed her phone. "Marty—you seeing this?" she asked one of her tech guru's buried in another room.

"All over it, boss. Already copying every single piece of data. A couple of the servers have ten terabytes on them. We'll have our own systems running this stuff all night. It's a huge bingo. I've also got the history on every one of these—even the ones they think they erased. Give me a day or two and I'll have his entire life story including financials for you."

"Outstanding." She hung up with him and called Eric Chow in another tech room. "Eric, you catching anything from the new target?"

"Hell, yeah. We're five by five—clear as a bell. Recording multiple calls already. Everything will be run for hidden codes. Hey, if you're interested, they have three televisions watching Al Jazeera and one watching porn, which I think is illegal in the Kingdom. They cut off your hand for stealing; what do they cut off for watching porn?" He laughed.

Kim returned the laugh. "Great job, Eric. Log and copy everything. Anything real weird pops up, you call me any time of day or night on my cell."

"You mean like a goat showing up in the porn?"

"No, I said weird. I'm pretty sure goats and camels are fair game." She hung up and called Dex.

"Boss. We're in."

CHAPTER 23

Al Udeid Air Base

The team drove by bus from the prince's palace to their new home almost six hours away at Al Udeid Air Base in Qatar. With Doha coming up in the chatter on several occasions, it made more sense to stay there than in Riyadh. They could have arranged for a plane and a quick trip, but Mackey wanted everyone to see the terrain. Most of the drive was through dessert wasteland, with the occasional small village or smattering of farms that had irrigation systems.

"I changed my watch when we landed," said Cascaes to Mackey. "But I don't think I have the right century."

Mackey looked at the line of men on camels off in the distance and nodded. "Sure doesn't look like Iowa."

Chris looked out at the wasteland. "Doesn't look like *earth*. I'm guessing the crop dusting business isn't real big out here."

"Not so much. Besides, they have plenty of dust already."

Moose was sitting in the seat across the aisle from them. "Why is it that the most lethal amphibious fighting force in the world is in the middle of a fucking dessert?" he asked. He added, "Sir."

Mack laughed. "Because you go wherever the action is and you love it. If you need water to fight, I'll sprinkle some on you."

Moose gave him a thumbs up. "That's us. Instant ass kicking fighting force, just add water to activate."

The men eventually fell asleep as it grew dark. The bus rolled along for hours of highway. When they reached Qatar, the driver put on the lights inside the bus, and a Qatari border guard boarded the bus. Mackey spoke to him for a while, showed him his documents, and was allowed through the small border crossing.

They reached Al Udeid forty minutes later, a beacon of lights in the middle of more nothingness. With over 10,000 US military personal, it was a busy place. The Marine Tactical Electronic Warfare Squadron 3 was stationed there, and their EA-6B Prowlers were backed into bombproof hangers along the runway. A large sign read "Moon Dogs" with a motto underneath, "Not seeing is believing." The Marine air element was tasked with conducting airborne electronic warfare, day or night, in all weather, to support the Marine Ground-Air Task Force. These days, they were flying missions in Afghanistan.

Earl Jones walked up the aisle and stood near Mackey and Cascaes. "Jarheads? Shit! You said airbase, I was thinking Air Force. Then I knew we'd have a nice hooch. This is a *Marine* Air Wing—we might as well sleep outside."

"It won't be so bad. The Qataris are happy to have us here. The accommodations will be just fine. Besides, I'm hoping we'll be out working soon."

Raul Santos, another Marine Recondo yelled from his seat. "No man, Earl's hardcore. He needs to sleep outside. Keep him tough."

Earl gave him the finger.

Raul looked at Eric, the only other Marine. "You see that, man? No respect."

Earl looked back at Mackey. "Hey, skipper, what's a Moon Dog?"

Mackey laughed. "Electronics warfare squadron. Just a nickname. The third squadron does electronic jamming. When you jarheads were humping around in A-Stan, the Prowlers were flying overhead knocking out all the cell phones so the hajjis couldn't make a call and set off an IED. They also take out enemy radar and disrupt communications."

Earl nodded and grumbled. "*Jar heads*. Food's gonna suck."

Eric was looking out the window. "This country is a shitty place for a sniper," he mumbled, half to himself. He didn't like any place that didn't offer high ground with concealment. Wide open rolling wasteland could be used to hide, but it made for lousy line of sight.

Raul shook his head. "Friggin country boy—always looking for someplace to hide and whack somebody."

Eric looked at him and shrugged.

$\oplus$

The bus pulled up in front of a large building that looked like every other building. A Marine staff sergeant was there to greet them. On the side of the building was another sign. In big red letters, under the Marine Corps Globe and Anchor, was written:

WE STOLE THE EAGLE FROM THE AIR FORCE, THE ANCHOR FROM THE NAVY, AND THE ROPE FROM THE ARMY.

ON THE SEVENTH DAY WHILE GOD RESTED, WE OVERRAN HIS PERIMETER, STOLE THE GLOBE AND WE'VE BEEN RUNNING THE WHOLE SHOW EVER SINCE.

The men piled out of the bus and stretched. They were still dressed in their white Navy All Star sweat suits, with the red and blue stars and stripes design. Mackey said hello to the staff sergeant, who offered to lead them down to their sleeping quarters. They had been given a wing upstairs on the second floor that was separated from the rest of the Marine detail housed there.

"General Gallo says your team gets the royal treatment. Whatever you need that we can supply is yours. You guys played the Saudis today?"

"Yeah. A prince out there, with his personal billion dollar stadium. He even brought in ringers from the states," said Mackey.

The young Marine grimaced. "Didn't go well, huh?"

"Fuck that. We kicked his ass," said Mackey.

"Ooohhh Rrrraaaa!" replied the Marine with a fist bump. "Outstanding, sir. You need anything, pick up a phone and dial twenty-five. That's either me or my staff. Whatever you need. Mess opens at oh-five hundred because of the early flyers. It's two buildings over, the green door. Good night, sir."

The team started checking out the rooms. They were typical nondescript quarters, with a bed, a small desk, one bureau, and a closet. They were new and spotless, and the men were too exhausted to complain. Within twenty minutes, all of them were fast asleep with orders not to wake the coach or face a firing squad.

CHAPTER 24

Al Hamaq

Rasheed and Jamal had driven from one small village to another. The first meeting was to switch from their own car to an oversized van that had two large suitcases of cash in the back. Unlike the first driver, these men knew exactly what they were transporting and would be part of the planned attack in the coming weeks. The first attempt had failed—they would not. Both men were armed with knives, Glock pistols, and AK47s.

They arrived at Al Hamaq at eight in the morning, after driving three hours through the dessert sunrise. It was a tiny village of forgotten stone houses and buildings. The buildings were made out of the same stone that surrounded the village, and everything was the same reddish-brown color as far as the eye could see. There were very few signs of life, and their large vehicle was the only thing in the village that wasn't a thousand years old.

Twenty minutes after they arrived, three black SUVs pulled into the village and drove to the field where they had parked their van. One door opened and a man appeared in white robes and sunglasses.

"You have the money?" he asked bluntly.

The driver, Rasheed, said yes.

"You will follow us."

The man ran back to his car and the truck tore off, kicking up dust. Rasheed took off after him, and the two other SUVs pulled up behind them. The four vehicles sped along Highway 10 until they reached a small turnoff that led to the farm where Tariq had met his fate.

The vehicles came to a stop by the small house, and men quickly emptied out of the SUVs with AK47s, rushing to Rasheed and Jamal, who instinctively grabbed their own weapons. After two minutes of excited screaming from every man in the courtyard, the outnumbered couriers placed their weapons on the ground. They were thoroughly searched, and their pistols and knives were taken from them, as well as their cell phones.

Two men grabbed the suitcases out of the back of the van, and the other two men were pushed along at gunpoint through the house to the rear courtyard where Abu Mohamed sat waiting. His face showed his displeasure at having been made to wait the extra two days for his fifty million dollars.

Abu looked at one of his men and motioned with his chin. The man opened the two large suitcases and looked inside. Bundles of American hundred dollar bills were packed like bricks inside each case. Fifty million dollars took up a lot of space. He nodded.

Abu Mohamed stood and walked around the table to the two nervous men. "You don't work directly for the man responsible for making me wait and will not be held accountable. Come."

Abu walked out of the courtyard and crossed a small field with the two men and a few bodyguards following close behind. They walked to a small barn and the men opened the door. Inside was the wooden crate that had taken a journey from Syria to Lebanon to Egypt to this small Saudi farm. Abu Mohamed didn't know where it was headed and didn't care. He knew the men's association with Jihadist radicals and any target they chose would be fine with him.

Rasheed and Jamal walked to the crate and saw the crowbars laid on top of it. Abu nodded when they looked at him for permission. The two of them worked together carefully to remove the end of the crate, prying and pulling ever so gently. Together, they removed the wooden end, revealing a large aluminum bomb that sat strapped into a metal cart with hydraulic wheels. Heavy straps and chucks prevented the cart from moving, and the two men worked to remove the encumbrances. When the cart was free, they pulled it out. The special wheels made it possible for two men to move the seven hundred pounds. This same type of system was used to roll the munitions under a jet's wing to be loaded for a bombing mission.

"I need to look inside," said Rasheed nervously.

"Why? You don't trust me?" asked Abu.

"Fifty million dollars is a lot of money. And I'm responsible for delivering the Sarin. I mean no disrespect."

Abu pointed to a red metal box on the side of the barn. "There are tools there if you wish to open it."

The two men walked over and pulled out screwdrivers, then returned to the large bomb. They carefully removed the twelve screws and then pulled off the plates on top of the deadly munition. Inside, a hundred round glass bomblets were stacked like grapes in a myriad of wires. The weapon had been designed to be dropped by plane, and then detonated above the enemy. The airburst would scatter the liquid into a fine spray mist which would kill in less than a few moments.

Jamal looked to Rasheed nervously. How could they know what they were looking at? "It looks like it, right?" he whispered to Rasheed.

Abu motioned to his men who were on the two immediately with their AK47s pushed into their chests. There were a few seconds of terrified confusion, and then Abu spoke.

"You say you mean no disrespect, and yet you keep me waiting three days for my money and have the nerve to question my integrity?" He barked orders at his men, who grabbed Jamal by the hair and pulled him to a post in the barn. They tied him against the pole so tightly he couldn't move his arms or legs at all. Rasheed was held at gunpoint.

Abu barked a few more orders, and one of his men carefully pulled off one of the glass balls. The men all moved away from Jamal, who was now begging to be released with tears running down his cheeks. Abu walked out quickly while his bodyguards pulled Rasheed behind them. The last man out, the one holding the Sarin bomblet turned when he got to the door and threw it as hard as he could at Jamal's chest. The glass shattered and sprayed him with the colorless, odorless liquid. Jamal's face began blistering immediately.

Rasheed and Jamal were both screaming as the men raced out of the barn, slamming the door behind them. Jamal's screaming went on for almost twenty seconds—a high pitched wail that pierced Rasheed's heart. The screaming turned into a bubbly gurgle, and then went silent.

Abu walked to Rasheed and stood almost nose to nose with him. "In fifteen minutes, you can go inside and tell me if it was Sarin or water in that weapon. I suggest you wait the fifteen minutes. And then you have another fifteen to get that in your van and get out of my sight before I put you next to your friend."

CHAPTER 25

Al Udeid

The team woke up leisurely and headed to the mess hall, a few at a time. No one woke Mackey, and the overall mood was that of "a day off"—a very rare occurrence. The SEALs were up early, along with Marine sniper Hodges, who had grown up on a farm and was always up before sunrise. The eight of them walked together over to the mess hall.

"Why ain't you sleeping in like the boss?" asked Hodges to Cascaes.

"You could have slept, why didn't you?" asked Chris.

He shrugged. "Must be the farm boy in me."

"Well, nothing wrong with hitting the ground running. Lots of pilots around here, I'm betting the food is good."

The men lined up with everyone else and filled trays with food from the buffet. Hodges had guessed correctly, and there was a huge selection, including grits and biscuits and gravy. Eric filled his plate with grits and mixed scrambled eggs into it. Then he poured gravy all over the biscuits.

"You do that on purpose?" asked Moose, staring in disbelief at the mess on Eric's plate.

"You never ate grits and eggs?"

Moose was still staring. "That would be a no. And what the hell did you do to your rolls?"

"Biscuits! Biscuits and gravy! I can't believe they have it here in Qatar! Feels like I'm home."

A young kid working behind the counter smiled at Eric and quietly said, "Quartermaster's from Georgia."

"Well, it's high cotton. I'm a happy man," said Eric.

"And I'm going to puke watching you eat," said Moose as he grabbed a stack of pancakes and a huge pile of bacon and sausage. Moose glanced over at Ripper's plate and saw the immense pile of food Ripper had stacked on his tray. "Jesus. Between country boy over here and your fat ass, I could really lose my appetite."

Ripper shrugged. "I don't see you worrying about your diet, Mr. Sausage-Bacon-Pancake Fatass."

"That really hurts, man," said Moose sarcastically. He then reached over and grabbed a sausage off of Ripper's plate, which he shoved in his mouth.

By the time the eight of them were finishing up, everyone else except Mackey had joined them for breakfast. The group relaxed and joked, enjoying the morning off. Mackey walked in just as they were all about ready to leave. They all said hello to the boss, who filled a plate and took a seat by Cascaes.

"You slept a long time," said Chris quietly. "I'm jealous. I forgot how to sleep late ten years ago."

"I wasn't sleeping. Been on the horn with Langley. It's going to get busy sooner than later."

"They have something solid?"

"Not exactly, but they're pulling a lot of intel from the bugs we dropped. When I finish eating, we'll take a few minutes and I'll catch you up."

CHAPTER 26

Al Hamaq

Rasheed sat on the hard ground sobbing outside the barn. Abu and a few of his men had left, leaving two guards with AK47s watching over the distraught man. After a while, one of the men commanded Rasheed to get up and open the doors, which he did.

After Rasheed pulled open the large barn doors, the men told him to wait another five minutes. Even from the doorway, Rasheed could see what was left of Jamal. His body was still tied to the pole, but he was as white as Abu's robes. The skin on his face had blistered to the point that he was unrecognizable. Foam was running out of his nose and gaping mouth, and his red eyes were wide open, not seeing anything. Quite simply, he was hideous.

Rasheed began praying. The two men ordered him inside after a few minutes, but stayed outside themselves. They waited until Rasheed approached Jamal's body and didn't die himself before they walked inside.

"Don't touch his clothes!" one of them yelled.

Rasheed looked back at them.

"The air is clear, but it stays on clothes and skin for a long time. Leave him. Take your crate and go."

"I can't leave him," said Rasheed.

"He's dead. If you touch him, you'll join him. Take your bomb and go."

Rasheed looked at Jamal one last time and then walked quickly to the hydraulic cart, straining as he pulled it out of the barn. The two men watched him a few seconds and then decided to help so they could get rid of him. They also didn't want him dropping any of the bomblets.

Between the three of them, they pushed and pulled the cart outside and told Rasheed to get his van, which he did. Once the rear doors were open, the cart was cranked up to the same height as the rear floor by way of a winch built into the cart, and the bomb was pushed off the rollers into the back of the van which creaked and dropped a centimeter or two. They threw a blanket from the back of the van over the huge weapon.

The men slammed the doors closed and grabbed Rasheed by his shirt. "You take that road back to the highway. If we ever see you again you're dead, you understand? Abu doesn't like the way you do business."

Rasheed threw the van into drive and drove off with tears in his eyes. He hated leaving Jamal, who had been willing to die for the Jihad, but wanted to die in battle like a martyr, not the way he had been wasted. He drove as smoothly as possible on the country road, taking it slow and steady. The bomb was sitting on the floor, secured only by its own weight. When he got to the highway, he made a right and headed east, slowly increasing his speed until he began to calm down. When he felt safe, he pulled out his disposable cell phone and pressed send.

Abdul Aziz, "Servant of the Powerful One," answered his phone. Abdul was the leader of a small sect of Wahhabi Jihadists operating inside Saudi Arabia with missions in Iraq, Afghanistan, and an occasional strike in Europe when possible. Only Rasheed had this particular phone number.

"Salam," he said quietly.

"I'm on my way," he said, sounding very distraught.

"What's wrong?" asked Abdul, always extremely cautious, especially when using a cell phone. He constantly scanned

the sky whenever he was about to make a call, fearful of the
dreaded drones.

"They killed Jamal!"

Abdul's face fell. "They double crossed us?" His face was
turning red under his white robe.

"I have the bomb, but Abu Mohamed was angry about
waiting for the money and was offended when I wanted to
make sure the Sarin was real. He used it on Jamal to prove it.
It was horrible to see."

"Get here as fast as you can."

"Two hours or so," said Rasheed. He hung up and prayed
for Jamal as he drove through the endless desert towards the
abandoned plant that served as headquarters for some of the
deadliest terrorists in the world.

CHAPTER 27

Al Udeid Air Base

Mackey and Cascaes were sitting in a small office near their barracks. It was typical military neat and very sterile. Beige paint had apparently been on sale when the contract had been awarded by the government. The rest of the team had been given the entire day off to do whatever they wanted. It sounded wonderful, except there was very little to do on the base, and it was over a hundred degrees outside with a wind that blew like a blast-furnace. Most of the men listened to music, cleaned weapons, wrote emails, Skyped with friends, or watched whatever was available on satellite television.

Mackey had a laptop and was opening up encrypted emails that included pictures of Middle Eastern men while speaking with Kim Elton and Dex Murphy back in Langley.

"Our techs have been pouring over a ton of communications and data from the bugs you set up. We're trying to create a picture of what's going on over there. It's alarming," said Kim.

"Alarming how?" asked Mackey.

"Well, here in the US, you can't deposit ten grand without a paper trail through the banking system. Prince Awadi's got huge cash deposits and withdrawals happening on a regular basis, and if we didn't have someone inside the bank, we'd never know about any of it. That fifty million you clipped must have been to finance whatever's going on over there, and there's a second withdrawal for the same amount a couple of

days later, which we assume is the replacement money. But we
still don't know what it's for. The smart money is on weapons
of mass destruction. No one needs fifty million to build a few
IEDs."

"Right, I think we assumed that from the start," said Mackey.

"There have been some rumors we're trying to follow up
on," said Kim tentatively. She looked at Dex, who nodded and
jumped in.

"Look, we don't work on guessing or conjecture. I like solid
intel before it gets passed around, but you guys are in the field.
We may need you to do some of the follow up yourselves,"
said Dex.

"Sure. What are you hearing?" said Mackey.

"Mack, for all I know it's total bullshit. But it's too scary
to ignore. You know the UN monitored the Syrians when they
took apart their chemical weapons stockpiles, but there's no
way to know if they ever got it all. Hell, there've been recent
Sarin attacks in Iraq and Afghanistan. The shit's coming from
somewhere, and the most likely culprits are Iraq and Syria. We
got word through the Israelis that a shipment of Sarin went
from Syria to Lebanon and then vanished. Supposedly, it was
a large weapon."

"Fifty million dollars worth?" asked Cascaes.

"Well, not fifty million to the guys who sell it the first time,
but after it passes through a few middlemen, who knows? Is
fifty million a fair asking price for something that can kill tens
of thousands of people?" replied Dex.

Chris and Mackey looked at each other. "Sarin?" asked
Chris out loud, to no one in particular. "What kind of delivery
systems were the Syrians using?"

Dex answered, "They had dumb bombs and artillery shells.
Similar to the Honest John types we were using back in the
sixties. Theirs are even more primitive. Glass bomblets inside
the shells."

Chris thought for a second. "So they could disassemble the thing and pass out a hundred or so smaller Sarin bombs for suicide bombers, bobby traps, IEDs; it wouldn't necessarily have to be a singular large scale event."

"The possibilities are endless," agreed Dex.

"So what can we do from our end?" asked Mackey.

"Right now, nothing. We're buying a lot of favors and squeezing where we can. I'm hoping we have a solid lead for you within a day or two."

"That's fast, what's going on?" asked Mackey.

"Bank cameras captured the images of the two guys who picked up the cash for the prince. The bank won't share that kind of information, but we have our guy inside. He's more worried about his own bank account, fortunately for us. We have facial recognition software working on it, as well as some local informants. If these two are important, we'll get some names and leads.

CHAPTER 28

Abandoned Oil Facility, Saudi Desert

Rasheed pulled into the compound slowly, and a man appeared from the shadows and opened the metal gate. The compound was a dinosaur skeleton in the desert—ancient, hulking, and dead, with giant metal machinery that had long rusted into oblivion. The cluster of buildings looked like they had been dropped in the middle of nowhere. Once inside the compound, Rasheed drove slowly into a large corrugated aluminum building. Perhaps once shiny and silver in the sun, the building was now brown and beginning to fall apart. He parked in the rear of the open structure and stopped the engine. Men began flowing into the building, excited and loud, screaming "God is great!" as they greeted their comrade, now a very important person, indeed.

Abdul Aziz appeared from the group of men, wearing a long white shirt and robes. His salt and pepper chin beard made a long point off his face like the evil genie in a child's cartoon. His mirrored sunglasses hid his dark, hate-filled eyes.

Rasheed stepped out of the van, into the hot stale air of the old building. It was over a hundred degrees, and there wasn't any hint of a breeze. At least the metal roof kept the sun off of them. Rasheed walked to the rear of the van and opened the door, then pulled off the blanket revealing the large bomb that filled the entire rear of the van. When the men saw it, they began praising Allah. Abdul walked straight to the van and greeted Rasheed, then looked inside at the bomb with great admiration. He quietly prayed for a moment, and then grabbed Rasheed by the arms excitedly.

"Jamal's death was not in vein! This weapon will change everything! God is great!" he screamed. The rest of the men in the building all cheered and repeated, "*Allahu Akbar!*"

After a moment of celebration, Abdul raised his hands and the crowd went silent. "We have preparations to make. Everything we do from here on must be done with great care. Any mistakes with the Sarin will kill all of us before we can complete God's will. Pay attention and follow instructions and, God willing, we will drive the Infidels from the Holy Lands."

CHAPTER 29

Mackey and Cascaes were back in Mackey's room talking to Langley on a video conference. Kim and Dex were obviously excited on their end of the phone.

"We've finally got something," announced Kim, the excitement showing in her face.

"Shoot," replied Mackey.

"The Bedouins, of all people, gave us a break. This is huge," said Kim.

"And these are folks who n*ever* talk to *anyone* about *anything*," interrupted Dex.

"So why now? You sure it's reliable?" asked Cascaes.

"Yes. Listen…these Bedouin tribesmen are moving through the desert by camel, and they come upon a body. Ninety-nine times out of a hundred, they'd just pass it and not say a word. But *this* body is so disturbing in appearance, and has a pair of dead Golden Jackals next to it, that they decide to notify the authorities," said Kim.

"I'm not sure I'm following," said Mackey. "Dead jackals?"

"Yes. That's what made them stop and look closer. The jackals found the body and opted for a quick meal. They had a lick or two and dropped dead. The body was very blistered and chemically burned—not sunburned. A few of the Bedouins had seen the effects of Sarin gas before, probably in Iraq, although I'm not sure about that part. Anyway, they knew the jackals had died from trying to eat the bodies, proving to them, in their

114

minds, that something was very wrong. They decided to call it in to the Saudi authorities."

"So these tribesmen just happened to have a phone?" asked Mackey skeptically.

"Yes. And satellite television on flat-screens inside their tents. They're Bedouin, not Amish. They even sent a few photos of the body with the GPS location—the body had been dumped in the desert, far from any town or road. If the jackals hadn't been digging around the body, I doubt they'd have spotted it or called it in. Anyway, the Saudis sent a team and recovered it. Lab tests confirmed Sarin residue, and fingerprints got a match."

The word Sarin hung in the air like the poison itself.

"A match to whom?" asked Mackey.

"A suspected terrorist from the New Wahhabi Jihad. He was just a low level soldier, but he was being watched. A guy named Jamal Salam. He was being looked at in a few bombings. But here's where it all starts to come together. Remember I told you we had video from the bank that our facial recognition software was working on? Well, the fingerprints and video matched. Jamal Salam, the dead body in the dessert, is also one of the two men that withdrew fifty million dollars for Prince Awadi."

"Holy shit," said Cascaes quietly.

"Wait, it gets a lot better," replied Kim. "Your bugging devices picked up a call from a disposable cell phone to Prince Awadi. Then a call from Awadi *back* to the cell a few minutes later, and then a *video* from the cell back to Awadi."

"What kind of video?" asked Mackey, his furrowed face showing his interest.

"An execution video. *This* is the prize," said Kim, her heart pounding in her chest. "In the video, a man decapitates Tariq Fareed. Tariq is NWJ for sure, but that's not the big news. The man who murdered him in the video is the big fish—Abu Mohamed."

"Wait a second," said Cascaes. "This Tariq guy, was he the other guy at the bank with Jamal?"

"No, we'll get to that in a second. Abu Mohamed is one of the largest illegal arms dealers in the Middle East. We've been after him for five years, but the guy is very careful. If anyone could get Sarin from Syria, it would be him. Now, based on the video, we believe that Tariq was meeting Abu Mohamed to make the pickup of the Sarin. The fifty million that you intercepted put a wrench in the deal, and Mohamed took it out on Tariq. You with me?"

Mackey and Chris both nodded automatically. "Who was at the bank with Jamal?" asked Cascaes again.

"We've confirmed the identity of the other man as Rasheed Rawani, a Saudi national known to be a member of the New Wahhabi Jihad. He's been on our radar since the Embassy bombing in Riyadh last year. If he's alive, our guess is *he's* where you find the Sarin."

"Not Abu Mohamed?" asked Chris.

"Mohamed is an arms dealer, not a soldier. If he brought in Sarin, it was to sell, not to use. Now, if he was as pissed at Rasheed as he was at Jamal or Tariq, then Rasheed's dead, too, and Abu Mohamed still has the Sarin. Or, if the deal went down with the second fifty million, then Abu Mohamed is in the wind again with a big bag of cash, and Rasheed Rawani has a very big bomb somewhere in Saudi."

They were all silent for a moment. "But you don't think the target is in Saudi?" asked Chris.

"Hard to say with any certainty, but the rumors and chatter we've been picking up reference Doha, Qatar, not Riyadh."

"Why not warn Qatar and let them step up border patrol?" asked Chris.

Dex and Kim looked at each other. "Chris, you're still thinking like an American," said Dex. "If we warn the Qataris, most likely it gets back to Abu Mohamed or Rasheed Rawani, and they just pick a different target or work a way around border security."

"Great allies," replied Chris quietly.

"So what's the play?" asked Mackey.

Kim's face showed great intensity. "Remember I told you that we had the execution video. Iphone pictures and videos contain GPS information. We know the exact location of where Tariq was executed. Had it been in a city, we'd figure they had quickly moved to a different safe house; but this is a very remote location. We think we found Abu Mohamed."

She let that sink in. "Mack, we've been after him for *five years*. This is the closest we've ever been. We need your team to go check it out."

"We're not talking a baseball game," said Mackey.

Dex interrupted. "No baseball. Covert assault on a hostile target. And Mack, there's a chance the Sarin is still there."

"That's comforting," he replied.

"We've looked at the layout of the compound. It's a farm with a couple of houses and barns. We're getting a drone over it now to try and get a head count."

"What are you thinking?" asked Cascaes.

"Similar assault to how we got Bin Laden. We bring you in with stealth choppers, drop you nearby, and let you hit the house at oh-four hundred when everyone's asleep. Night vision and surprise should get you in and out quickly. The Moon Dogs can fly what appears to be a routine flight from Doha to Riyadh. They take the scenic route and jam all electronics in the area of the compound along the way. It will cover the choppers in and out and also prevent any electronic detonations, in case the Sarin's wired."

Cascaes sighed. "We crashed a chopper in the Bin Laden raid. It all sounds so simple. Like stealing fifty million from a fruit truck."

Kim leaned forward towards the camera, her face almost glowing with her energy. "Chris, you have one of the best teams of Special Operators ever assembled. We have a slim chance of taking down Abu Mohamed and grabbing a Sarin bomb, if it's still there. Even if the Sarin is gone, Mohamed may know where it went. This is it. Our big break. We need you to get it done."

"Yes, ma'am," he replied.

Dex cleared his throat. "There's another wrinkle." He paused. "You'll be operating in Saudi Arabia, one of our strongest allies in the region, without their knowledge or permission. If something goes wrong, it will present an extremely difficult position for the administration. You won't be wearing official uniforms, not that anyone wouldn't know in two seconds you're Americans."

"So we're on our own," said Cascaes bluntly.

Dex looked uncomfortable. "Look—you get in, you ghost the bad guys, grab the Sarin if it's there, and get out. You'll be ex-filled to Doha."

"What if the Sarin *is* there?" asked Mackey.

"If it's there, it's going to be too heavy and dangerous to move. You'll blow it in place."

"Better be a long fuse," said Chris.

"Roger that," said Mackey. He looked at Dex on his screen. "So when do we go?"

"Tonight. We've got to move fast. We have our special operations folks putting together flight plans and coordinating aircraft, drones, and time tables. I know it doesn't give you enough time to prepare…"

"It doesn't give us *any* time to prepare!" snapped Chris.

"Give me three hours. You'll have satellite images of the target, a head count, and all of the details. It's not ideal. It's what we have."

"Understood," replied Mackey. "We'll be ready." He stared at Cascaes.

Cascaes looked at Mackey and nodded. "Yes, sir. We'll be ready."

Mackey pressed "end" and closed the laptop. He looked at Cascaes and raised his eyebrows.

"You caught the end of that. We're in Saudi Arabia. We get pinched, and it's a *difficult situation for the administration*. That means that Randall Hill is up their ass again. They'll scrub the team and scatter us into the breeze."

"Look on the bright side, Chris. We'll probably all die from the Sarin," said Mackey with a huge toothy grin.

Cascaes was in no joking mood. "We're going to take them down, and then I'm going to personally shove that Sarin bomb up Hill's ass." He stood up, added, "sir", and left.

CHAPTER 30

Abandoned Oil Facility, Saudi Desert

Morning prayers were finished. Abdul Aziz brought Rasheed to a small office inside their compound away from the others.

"It is time to strike, Rasheed. We will hit two places that will send a clear message to the Infidels. I will be leading the first attack. I need someone to lead the second attack—someone I can trust, who will not fail." He placed his hand on Rasheed's forearm and squeezed. "You brought us the weapon. You will be my general for the second strike."

Rasheed bowed his head humbly. "Thank you, Abdul. I would be honored."

"I haven't shared all of the details with the others. They are good soldiers, but they don't need to know yet." He paused and looked into Rasheed's dark eyes. "Manchester United is playing Spain in the emir's stadium. There will be tens of thousands of spectators, most of them foreigners. You've seen the pictures of that stadium. The emir invites westerners to drink alcohol and dress like whores. It's disgraceful."

"How will we carry it out?"

Abdul smiled and stood up, then walked to a closet. He pulled out an aluminum box with a canvas belt attacked to it. At first, Rasheed didn't understand what he was looking at. When he realized it was a vending box used by the workers in the stadium, the smile crept across his face.

"This is the prototype. They are being prepared as we speak. Eighty boxes will be armed with a Sarin bomblet and small detonation device. When it nears halftime, and the stadium is full, our soldiers will spread throughout the stadium with the boxes, selling food and drink. I will make one call, which will go to every phone detonator. The eighty boxes will explode at once, releasing enough Sarin to inflict massive casualties. Our martyred brothers will have stuck the Infidels on international television. The whole world can watch it happen, God willing."

Rasheed nodded. "It is an excellent plan, Abdul."

"It is only one part. While our men are spreading throughout the stadium, you will lead three others, each with your own car. The lead car will have enough explosives to take out the gate at Al Udeid and kill the guards. With them out of the way, the other three vehicles can attack the barracks there. I have a diagram that shows the locations of the barracks where their pilots live. These are the men that have been bombing our brothers in Iraq and Afghanistan for years. You will kill them all, God willing."

Rasheed bowed his head again. "To be the one who strikes the American airbase is a great honor, Abdul."

"Paradise will await us both."

The two of them returned to the large garage where three of the men were working on the preparations. They had carefully removed the bomblets from the bomb and were carefully packing them in Styrofoam. The Styrofoam was then wrapped with heavy duct tape, and a small amount of Semtex with a blasting cap and phone was then wired to it. The small bundle was then placed inside the bottom of the vendor box, which had been provided by a true believer who worked for the company. They would be switched out on game day morning, filled with food or beverages, and then sent out to the crowd according to the plan.

"As soon as they are finished, we will move from here. We need to get into Qatar as soon as possible. Your four vehicles have already been prepared. The first one is the truck. It contains enough Semtex to take out their concrete reinforced guardhouse. The three smaller cars have the Sarin. All of the vehicles have the explosives hidden inside the rear quarter panels. Even if the car was stopped and someone gave it a quick inspection, they would find nothing."

The preparations continued throughout the morning, and by Zuhr prayers at noon the vehicles were loaded and ready. Abdul called all of his men together in the warehouse, where they prayed together, and then he made a short speech to inspire his followers. Three cars would follow Rasheed north on Highway 75, the rest of the men would take several trucks and cars and head due east to Qatar via Highway 10. Both routes would be traveling through the eastern desert. They would space themselves out to avoid any possible suspicion, but the area was so remote that the odds of anyone bothering them were slim.

The vendor boxes were in a truck from the vending company that had been loaned to one of their members by a NWJ supporter inside the company. Of course, that person had no idea that the stadium was the target and he would most likely be killed for his assistance during the attack. The truck would be driven to the stadium where the vendor boxes would be brought into the catering area and then would be loaded with snacks and drinks. All of their paperwork was in order, although much of it was forged. Abdul Aziz and several of his men were traveling under false passports, but they were so well made, with the assistance of supporters inside the Saudi passport office, that they would pass any inspection.

The vehicles pulled out of the old facility a few at a time, a caravan of sorts, and drove out into the one hundred degree Saudi sunshine.

CHAPTER 31

Al Udeid Hanger, 1900 Hours

The brass in Special Operations back in Washington, DC loved code names. They named this one Silent Serpent, and in very short order had coordinated a very complicated mission with the Special Operations people from Al Udeid airbase and the CIA.

Mackey and Cascaes had assembled their team, with all of their gear, in Al Udeid's helicopter hanger. With the two space-aged looking UH-60A stealth Black Hawks serving as dramatic backdrop, Mackey began the briefing. A screen behind Mackey showed a satellite image of the farm compound they would be assaulting.

"Gentlemen, it's time to earn your reputation. You're meat-eaters tonight. This farm is the last known location of an illegal arms dealer named Abu Mohamed. It's believed that he's smuggled in Sarin from Syria, which is to be supplied to New Wahhabi Jihad terrorists for an impending attack. We don't know what their attack plans are yet, but if we can hit the target and destroy the Sarin, we'll stop it before it starts." He pressed a button on the remote and the projector showed a grainy picture of Abu Mohamed. "This is Abu Mohamed. We'd like to take him alive if possible. If the Sarin's already been moved, he may be able to tell us where it went. Anyone else in the compound is considered an armed threat. We'll be using silenced weapons and night vision when we assault at oh-four hundred. Our goal is to get in, take out everything that moves, confirm the Sarin, and destroy it. We then exfil to Doha on the same birds that brought us in."

Mackey pointed to the two strange looking Blackhawks behind the team. "These are the same type of birds that were used to get Bin Laden. They'll be bringing us in. Dust off is at oh-three hundred. Time to target is one hour. The Moon Dogs will be flying two Prowlers from Al Udeid to Riyadh, which isn't unusual. Routine training flight, except this time they'll loop south and jam all radar and electronics in the area. Our birds will go in quiet and invisible. The Prowlers will be jamming everything at the farm. No phones, alarms, or detonation devises will be operational. In theory, our comm channel won't be affected, but if we lose ears with each other, follow the timetable and make sure you know where each other are. Birds will drop us fifty yards from the target so we won't wake anyone up. Hodges will find a spot nearby to provide sniper cover. Hodges, you'll be silencing that canon."

"Yes, sir. At fifty yards the silencer's range limitation won't be a factor. Looks like there's a little spot near the infil point that might work," said Hodges, pointing to a rocky outcropping.

Mackey pressed the remote and showed a closer image of the two small houses and large barn. "Cascaes will lead team one into the larger farmhouse. Moose, Ripper, Jensen, McCoy, Stewart, Santos, and Smitty—you're team one. I'll take team two into the barn. It's the most likely place to keep the Sarin. The bombs are heavy. Not the kind of thing you carry into the living room. Team two is Perez, Cohen, O'Conner, and Woods. We'll all be in chemical suits. We move through nice and slow, eliminate all targets, and secure the bomb if it's there. The chem-suits are just a precaution, but once we confirm the Sarin, we're blowing it in place, not taking it with us. Ernie P., I know how you love blowing shit up. Make sure you have enough C-4 and a long-ass fuse. We don't want to be anywhere near that Sarin when it detonates. Jones and Koches are team three. You'll get that small building in the back. Satellite and drone intel confirms at least six Hajjis have been in and out of the main house. We haven't seen activity in and out of the barn or smaller house, but that doesn't mean no one's there. If we do this right, we're through the doors at oh-four hundred and dusting off twenty minutes later."

Cascaes stood up and walked to Mackey. "We're going in unrehearsed, but this should be a straight forward mission. This is sensitive, gentlemen. We're taking down targets on an ally's soil without their permission. This is not an official operation. The birds will be on the ground waiting for us to get out and dust off. Prowlers can't stay on station more than twenty minutes without raising questions. We move silent and efficiently. Hodges, you're going to be alone out there on overwatch. Watch your six, and make sure you get your ass to the chopper when it's time to go. Team one is on chalk one—teams two and three on chalk two. For now, we stay here in the hanger until it's time to go. Check comms and weapons, eat some delicious MREs, rack out, and be ready to haul ass."

CHAPTER 32

Qatar, Sunset

Abdul Aziz thanked Allah for seeing him through the border crossing without incident. The caravan of cars had arrived a few at a time at the small warehouse located only a couple of kilometers from the stadium. They had driven past it on their way to the new safe house, and Abdul had felt his heart pounding in his chest when he saw the stadium for the first time. It was a massive structure and would be filled with so many Infidels. He felt immense pride in his choice of targets.

Once they arrived at the warehouse, the men ate a simple meal of food they had brought with them, and unrolled bedding that had been left for them at the warehouse. They would sleep and try to keep focused on their mission and eternal reward. They fought off any of their hidden personal fear with inspirational images of their leader, Abdul Aziz, leading them into Paradise. Abdul had failed to mention to his men, including Rasheed, that he had no intention of dying with the rest of them. He was too important. He would get everyone into position, leave the stadium, and make the call from a safe distance.

Once the men were settled in for the night, Abdul called Rasheed on a new disposable cell phone.

"Assalamu Alaykum Wa Rahmatullaahi wa barakato," said Rasheed quietly from a small motel.

"Wa alaykum assalam," replied Abdul. "You are safe?"

"Yes. A small motel in a remote location. An hour from the target. Everything is fine. The vehicles are right outside our rooms. We're watching them. I don't think there are any other guests at this motel. I await the final instructions."

"Excellent. The match begins tomorrow night at six o'clock. You will attack at seven, so the stadium here is already full. We will attack shortly after you. Our attacks must be close together."

"We'll meet again in Paradise," said Rasheed, thinking about his friend Jamal.

"God willing," said Abdul, even though he wasn't planning on being in Paradise for quite a while yet.

CHAPTER 33

Al Udeid, 0300 Hours

The men had woken up from a few hours of uncomfortable sleep on the hangar floor and quickly packed up their gear. They hustled to the stealth Black Hawks and took their positions inside. The crew chief gave the pilot a thumbs-up, and the pilot radioed the hanger security officer to open the hangar doors. The massive doors slowly slid open, and the pilots started their rotors. Only the SEALs had ever been on stealth helicopters before, and the rest of the team was amazed at how quiet they were. The machines moved forward and lifted off out of the hangar with only the slightest of sub-woofer background noise.

The two Black Hawks rose and banked southwest staying fairly low at 2,000 feet. Once they were over the desert, they dropped even lower and flew at 150 knots towards their target. Thirty minutes after they took off, two Moon Dog prowlers blasted down the runway and shot off into the moonless night. They hit 500 knots at an altitude of 25,000 feet only a moment later. By the time the birds were approaching the target, the Prowlers would be high overhead, making sure that the birds were invisible, and that no one on the ground could detonate any explosives electronically.

The pilot's voice on the lead helicopter spoke quietly into the crew chief's headset. "Time to target, sixty seconds, over."

"Roger, sixty seconds, over." The crew chief yelled at Mackey, who had a full chemical suit on with night vision goggles over it. It was cumbersome. "Sixty seconds!" he yelled at Mackey, who gave him a thumbs-up. The rest of the men returned the hand signal.

The two helicopters touched down gently on the sand, the doors slid open, and the men jumped down and began moving quickly towards the compound, except Hodges, who hustled towards the rocky tower about halfway between the landing zone and the compound. He climbed quickly to the top of the rocks and began settling into sniper mode.

Cascaes' team moved single file towards the farmhouse. The area was silent. Only the sounds of their boots crunching across baked ground made any noise. The laser sites on their M4s made red dots on the door of the house as they approached. Cascaes looked at Moose and Ripper, who instantly moved around the back of the house to find the rear door.

Mackey and his four-man team moved to the barn, looking like aliens in their chemsuits and night vision. Cohen carried a small sniffing device in his left hand that would alert them to any Sarin in the air. In his right was a silenced Beretta. The rest of them carried M4s.

Jones and Koches slipped silently over a stone wall and headed to the small house in back of the farmhouse.

High overhead, the Moon Dogs were screwing up cell phone service for anyone within ten miles who might be awake at four in the morning.

"In position," whispered Moose from the rear door of the main house.

"Go quiet," replied Cascaes. He turned the doorknob slowly and pushed. It was bolted from the inside. So much for a quiet entrance. He stepped to the left and Raul Santos kicked the door as hard as he could below the knob. The old wooden door splintered, and the door flew open. McCoy, Stewart, Smitty, and Cascaes piled into the room. Santos took a knee and checked behind them. From the rear of the house, Moose and Ripper shattered their door and moved up a flight of stairs immediately in front of them.

In the front of the house, a guard was sleeping on a couch near the door. He woke up when the door was kicked open, but by the time he reached for his AK47, he had been double-tapped by McCoy right through his heart. They all hesitated and listened. Still no sound.

Moose and Ripper reached the top of the stairs and stepped into a small hallway. There were two doors on each side of the hall. Moose took the first one on the right and Ripper the first on the left. They each entered quietly. Moose found himself in an empty bedroom and backed out. Ripper was also in a bedroom, where a man was fast asleep. It didn't give him any pleasure to kill a defenseless man, but Ripper put two rounds through the man's head after making sure it wasn't Abu Mohamed.

He backed out into the hallway and nodded to Moose, and the two of them walked to the next two doors.

⊕

Out by the barn, Ernie P. slowly pulled the barn door open while the rest of the team had guns at the ready. Jon Cohen held out the sniffing device but didn't get any reading. "It's safe," he whispered. Mackey stepped into the barn with Lance Woods. A quick scan proved to them that they were in a large empty barn.

"Shit," mumbled Mackey. "Search thoroughly. Check for cellars and look up the stairs in the loft."

The team moved quickly, rummaging through every possible hiding place and coming up empty.

"Hey," whispered Jon to Mackey. He pointed to a large empty crate. "No reading on the crate, but there's maybe a trace by that pole. Maybe they spilled some a few days ago. Barely registers but there *was* Sarin in this barn."

Earl Jones and Jake Koches moved quickly across a small courtyard to the rear house. Jake signaled that he was going around the front. Earl nodded and moved around the corner looking for the back door. As he turned the corner, he found himself face to face with a teenage boy, maybe sixteen or so, holding an old shotgun. The boy raised the shotgun and Earl just stared at him. Images of the kids in the truck cab flashed in his brain and he froze. In his earpiece he could hear Eric Hodges yelling at him.

"Earl!"

The shotgun blast threw Earl almost three feet onto his back. A split second later, Hodges fired a round that took off the top of the kid's head.

"Overwatch to team three, Jones is down!"

Jake Koches had just gotten to the front door when he heard the blast, and he kicked the door open and bolted into the house. The tiny stone house was only one floor, with two rooms separated by a knee wall. Abu Mohamed had been sleeping on a couch in the rear part of the house when the shotgun woke him up. He grabbed his AK47 and pointed it at Koches, who fired two quick rounds through his chest and then a second two through his head from across the house. He raced through the rest of the house checking for other hostiles, desperately trying to get out the back door to Earl Jones. Jake made sure the rooms were clear and then opened the rear door, taking a knee and looking around the courtyard. He saw the dead kid and scanned the yard. Nothing. He moved quickly out of the house and found Earl on his back coughing.

"Earl!" he yelled as he dropped to his knee. In his earpiece, Hodges spoke quietly. "Jake, I've got you covered. Rear yard is clear."

"Earl?" repeated Jake, grabbing Earl's Kevlar vest. The shotgun blast had hit him square in the chest. The ceramic plate over Earl's heart had stopped three of the four slugs, and the fourth had gone through Earl's right bicep without hitting any bone or artery.

"I'm good. I'm okay," said Earl, dazed.

Jake pulled a pressure bandage out of his cargo pant pocket and tied off Earl's arm. "The house is clear. I took out one hostile, but I think it was the target. Let's boogie to the bird." He helped Earl to his feet, retrieved Earl's weapon, and the two of them jogged back to the Black Hawks. "Skipper, team three is exfil. Target is KIA, over."

Mackey was still in the barn when he heard Koches. There was no Sarin and now no one to ask about it. "All right, that's it. Team two is out. We go through the rear house on the way out. I need a picture of the KIA over there. Team one, you clear?"

Inside the house, upstairs, Ripper and Moose answered the question with repeated bursts from their M4s. "We're clear." Cascaes and the men downstairs waited for Ripper and Moose to come down the steps, and then the eight of them ran back towards the helicopters.

Mackey and his team took a quick picture of what was left of Abu Mohamed and then raced back to the extraction zone. "Hodges! Get your ass back to the bird!"

Two minutes later, two Black Hawks silently flew across empty desert back to Qatar airspace.

CHAPTER 34

Langley

Dex had spoken to Mackey and Cascaes after they landed back in Qatar. They were all disappointed at missing the Sarin and losing the opportunity to interrogate Abu Mohamed, but at least the world had one less illegal arms dealer peddling death. After the debriefing, Dex went home and showered and slept for five hours. When he returned to the office, his mind was racing. He called Kim.

"You wanted to see me?" asked Kim as she walked into Dex Murphy's office. "Morning. Have a seat. I think I might have an idea about the Qatar target."

"Something other than Al Udeid?" she asked.

"I was reading a week's worth of newspapers last night after living *here* all month. I came across a story about FIFA."

"FIFA? Like the video game my son plays?" she asked.

"No, the actual Football Federation. Soccer, whatever. So listen—the Emir of Qatar is a huge soccer fan, right? He builds this new high-tech, air-conditioned stadium and allows alcohol in the special sports fan zone to attract an international soccer crowd. He *really* wants the big games played in his country. So, the Executive Committee of FIFA decides where the World Cup is played every year. Qatar is getting the big game. Coincidently, the guy that runs the executive committee has a ten-year-old daughter who magically has two million dollars put into her bank account right before the decision is announced."

Kim nodded. "Yeah, now that you mention it, I think I remember hearing about that a few weeks back. It isn't a new story. But the Qatari World Cup isn't for another few years."

"Right—not until 2022. I'm not saying that this is about the World Cup, but it just made me think about the stadium. I looked at their schedule. Man U is playing Spain in two days. Those teams will pack the stadium. The stadium holds 45,000 plus. Would make for a helluva target, and the game will be broadcast live. If the NWJ wanted to make a big splash, that would do it."

Kim put her hand over her mouth. "Jesus. This whole time I was so focused on the airbase…"

"Not just you. We all were. But if they were to successfully detonate a Sarin bomb inside a packed stadium it would be a disaster."

Kim thought for a second. "Look, we don't trust the emir, but there's no way he'd allow this to happen in his stadium. He wants the big games, you just said so yourself. He wouldn't allow this to jeopardize the World Cup and the future of soccer for his country. We need to bring him into the loop. We'll need Qatari security to assist."

"Kim, when the target was our airbase, it was our problem. If it's the stadium, you're right, we'll share the intelligence, but it's *their* problem. Our guys don't run security for a foreign soccer stadium."

She frowned. "You're going to leave the safety of 45,000 fans to the Qatari police? They're going to need our help."

He shook his head. "It won't fly, Kim. We'll alert the emir, but that's it. The team doesn't get involved. I'm going to talk to the boss and tell him about this possibility. We still don't have anything solid that points to the stadium, just my crazy hunch."

"Your crazy hunch that I happen to *agree* with, Dex. We have to warn them immediately."

Dex called Kim back into his office right before the end of the day. It had been another exhausting day, working with the analysts who were still pouring through thousands of records trying to garner some information that might support their theory on the stadium attack.

When Kim entered Dex's office, she looked as exhausted as he did. "What's up?"

"POTUS called the emir, personally. After he told him about our theory and the possibility of Sarin being used, the emir called his security council together. The President suggested that maybe they cancel the game, but the emir asked the President if we'd cancel the Super Bowl because of a terror threat, and that was that. The emir is having his Security Council mobilize the army to help with gate security."

"The entire Qatari Army is what, 8,000 troops?" asked Kim.

Dex nodded. "They'll have 3,000 troops stationed all over the stadium, inside and out. They'll search everyone coming in."

"And if they blow the Sarin in the security line?" asked Kim.

Dex shrugged. "They'll do the best they can. They're not canceling the game. And the emir's right—we wouldn't cancel the Super Bowl."

"Our people are better at this, Dex."

"It's not going to happen. Save your breath. The boss spoke to the President, and the President says the emir is handling it. Thanked us for the tip. We're out of it."

Kim rubbed her eyes. "This sucks, Dex."

"Go home. Get some sleep, see your family, and take tomorrow off. Come in late on Thursday."

She stared at him coldly. "Just in time to watch Fox News cover the mass casualties at the stadium?"

"Go home, Kim."

She got up and headed out.

CHAPTER 35

Qatar

Wednesday was spent in prayer and meditation at the small motel. The men shaved their beards and heads and cleansed their bodies in preparation for martyrdom. Further south, Abdul's team was busier. Three of them had driven the truck to the stadium, and with the help of their coconspirator in the vending company, carefully smuggled in the loaded vendor boxes to the concession area. The phones had been fully charged, and the batteries would last a few days. The phones were all on, simply awaiting the call from Abdul Aziz that would change history.

As the men were leaving, they watched nervously as Qatari military trucks began arriving at the stadium. The men hurried back to Abdul at the warehouse and reported the sudden military activity.

Abdul listened and thought about it. He dismissed it as standard precautions. Besides, the bombs were already inside the stadium. It was too late for the army or anyone else to stop destiny.

When all the preparations were made, it was simply time to wait. Abdul's men prepared themselves, just as Rasheed's had, and spent the rest of the evening in prayer.

CHAPTER 36

Qatar, Thursday Morning

Rasheed and his men woke up with the sunrise—the last they would see on this earth. The sun was an orange ball of fire, illuminating the desert with long pink fingers across the sky. Rasheed wondered if it would look like this when the bombs went off. Would he hear anything? Feel anything? He smiled, and thought of the virgins who would be waiting for him.

The men prayed and wrote letters to family members, which would be left at the motel to be found by housekeeping some time after the attack.

At five o'clock, Rasheed, now the leader of this small group, rallied his men. "Brothers, we fear nothing. Allah the merciful will welcome us to Paradise as great warriors. Tonight, we'll drive to the base and catch the Americans at supper. While their pilots fill their fat bellies, Imad will drive the first vehicle into the gate and kill the guards, opening the road for all of us to follow." He looked at Imad. "Are you afraid, Imad?" he asked.

Imad puffed out his chest. "I have no fear! Allah shall welcome me to Paradise!"

Rasheed smiled and patted his shoulders. "Yes, Imad! *You* will inspire the attack! After Imad kills the guards, I'll drive the next car into the base. We drive through the entrance road, keep left, and head to the buildings. The barracks and dining hall are all in the same area. Watch for a building with

a green door. This is where they eat. This is where I shall go to
Paradise. If I'm successful, you will pick the closest barracks."

The other two nodded.

"In a few hours, we shall all meet in Paradise. There can be
no hesitation. No fear. Are you all ready?"

The three of them responded by chanting "God is great!"
and then the four of them headed to their vehicles. With
Imad in the lead car, the others stayed close behind as they
drove down the desolate road. Rasheed dialed Abdul on his
disposable cell phone.

Abdul greeted the only man who had his number.

"God is great," Rasheed replied calmly. "We're on the way.
Less than an hour. God willing, we will kill them all. I shall see
you in Paradise, my brother. "

"Blessings be upon you," replied Abdul. "You shall be
brave."

"I'm not afraid," said Rasheed, his voice quivering ever
so slightly. He hung up the phone and concentrated on the
red taillights in front of him. He would spend the next hour
praying as he drove.

CHAPTER 37

Al Udeid

Mackey and Cascaes assembled the team for an update. They all took seats around the conference table, including Earl Jones, his arm bandaged and resting in a sling where it would remain for another twenty-four hours.

"First things first," announced Mackey. "How are you feeling?"

Jones flashed his best fake smile and gave a thumbs-up with his left hand. "Hard core, Skipper. Thanks to my man, Hodges, I'm still on this side of the sod."

Mackey shot Eric a look. "Fine shooting, Hodges."

"Thanks, skipper," he replied calmly.

"What did the doc say?" Mackey asked Jones.

"Piece of cake, boss. Two weeks and I'll be doing one-armed pushups."

"That's what the doc said?" he asked suspiciously.

"No, doc says three or four weeks, but doc ain't never seen a 150th Street Recondo before."

Hodges and Santos, the other two Marines, both growled, "Ohhh Rraaah!" at that.

"Um hmm," grunted Mackey with a scowl. "Just keep me in the loop and let me know how you're doing. Now for the latest news on the Sarin and the NWJ. We spoke to Langley a dozen times over the past two days. Like I told you yesterday, the

Qataris are focusing on the soccer game tonight. They've got a few thousand soldiers and cops set up around the stadium, inspecting bags and keeping an eye on things. I hate sitting over here with my thumb up my ass while these psychos try and blow off a Sarin bomb in the middle of 45,000 people, but we've been ordered to stand down."

"So that's it?" asked Moose, obviously angry. "One of our guys almost gets ghosted in the raid, and then we get told to stay out of it?"

Cascaes snapped at his SEAL. "Stand down, Moose. We don't have to like it. Bottom line is, we ain't bouncers for the Qatari soccer stadium. Besides, it's not a hundred percent that's the target anyway. It's just one theory."

"What's the other theory?" asked Moose.

"That they're going to try and hit us right here. Al Udeid. Base commander's been alerted and the guards have been doubled up. Drones have been patrolling the airspace, Navy station at Doha is on high alert, and all military ships are under way to keep them out of port. Air force has been moving aircraft to bomb-proof bunkers or keeping them under heavy guard. This place is locked down pretty tight, but who knows. We wait and watch."

"That's so reassuring," said Moose.

Mackey looked around the room. "Al Udeid is in the middle of the desert. Anyone trying to get in is coming through a heavily defended gate. We're the Navy All-Star Baseball Team. We can't walk around base with commando gear. Sit tight and wait for orders. For now, stay here in the barracks. I want everyone close in case something comes up."

The team was dismissed, but Cascaes called Earl Jones back to wait a minute. Mack looked over, but Cascaes gave a quick shake of his head, and Mackey understood he wanted a private conversation. He walked out and closed the door behind him.

"How are you doing, Earl?" asked Cascaes.

Earl looked at him with a slightly annoyed face. "Like I told Mack, I'm good man. Just a scratch. I'll be G to G in two weeks."

Cascaes sat back and stared hard into his eyes. "I'm not talking about your arm, Earl."

Earl swallowed hard and stared back at him.

"You know what I'm talking about, Earl. How are you doing? You sleeping? Having nightmares?"

Earl looked up at the ceiling and around the room. He stood up. "I'm good, boss."

"Sit down," said Cascaes in a quiet voice that few fathers can master, but which command instant action. Earl sat.

"I'm good," he said, a little softer this time.

"Earl. There's no shame in getting help if you need it. There's people you can talk to if you're having a hard time dealing with something. The stress we deal with isn't normal. If you need to talk…"

Earl's eyes watered, and he cut Cascaes off. "What am I supposed to say to some shrink, Skipper? I blew away two little kids, and now I feel guilty about it? That gonna make it all better?" A tear ran down his face, which he quickly wiped away.

Cascaes exhaled slowly. "Look, man—I'm not saying talking about it makes it instantly better, but getting it off your chest helps, sometimes. I'm not religious, but I've seen plenty of my guys go to confession. You know what I think? I think the confession isn't about being forgiven by God. I think it's about being forgiven by *yourself.* You didn't murder two kids because you're some kind of sicko. You fired on an enemy vehicle to save *me*, Earl! You were trying to save my ass because that's what we do for each other. We kill and die for each other because we're a family. The kind of family that civilians won't ever understand. And right now, you need someone to have your back. When was the last time you had a real night's sleep?"

Earl stared at Cascaes through watery eyes and shrugged.

"Have you slept one good night since the ambush?"

Earl shook his head no.

"Listen, man—I'm not a psychiatrist, okay? But I've been in this shit for my entire adult life. Mack and I were just talking about this stuff. About the fact that we'll probably always be single because we're so fucked up after a whole life of doing this shit that we can't have normal conversations with women anymore. You're still young. You have to keep your head on straight. And there's more to it, Earl."

He paused and stared at Earl until Earl asked, somewhat timidly, "What?"

"If you don't get this shit squared away, you're going to get yourself or one of us killed. You hesitated out there, didn't you?"

Earl burst out crying without warning, and then covered his face with his hand. He'd been holding it in for too long, and when it came out, it didn't want to stop. Mackey stood and walked around the table, bent over, and gave Earl a hug, holding him for a moment until Earl composed himself.

"There's no shame in feeling sad or guilty over what happened, Earl. No shame. You got that? You're a bad-ass fucking warrior. I'll share my foxhole with you any day. But you can't just hold all this in until you explode. You need a few weeks for your arm to heal before you're ready to get to work, anyway. There's a doc on base you can talk to; I already asked."

Earl patted Cascaes' arm and Chris walked back around to his chair and sat. He leaned forward, his elbows on his knees, and looked at Earl. "Look, man, we've had more vets die from suicide than were killed in combat in the last ten years. Did you know that? It's fucked up, Jonesy. We get trained to become warriors and we kill and destroy and leave a wake of destruction behind us. And then we just get sent home and we're supposed to be able to go back to civilian life and be like everyone else. But we're not. And when you leave this family of guys that would kill or die for you, and you're all alone back in the world, you better be cool with everything you did over here. Because if you're not, you're going to be all alone at home—surrounded by people, maybe, but all alone. No one but your team knows what the deal is. So you need to find your peace *now*, Earl."

"I don't know why it hit me so hard, Skipper. I've been in plenty of combat before. Seen lots of shit. I just, I dunno…"

"They were kids, and you saw them up close and personal. You don't think I see them every day? I apologized to them. I apologized to God."

Earl looked at him confused. "You said you weren't religious?"

"I'm not. That doesn't mean I don't believe in God. Find me anyone who's been shot at that doesn't believe in *something*. My point is, I let it go. I apologized, and I forgave *myself*. And you need to find a way to do that. Otherwise, you're no good to yourself or anyone else. You're a good man, Earl. And a good Marine. I'm here if you ever want to talk." He reached into his pocket and pulled a card, which he slid to Earl. "This is the number for Doctor Hayes. I spoke to him briefly. Seems like a good guy. Anyway, you've got a couple of weeks off. Stop by and talk to him."

Earl slid the card into his pocket.

"It stays between us, Earl. But just so you know, the guys would all understand. And at some point, every single one of them should be talking to someone. Now get some sleep."

CHAPTER 38

Abdul's men traveled to the stadium a few at a time to report for work at the food concession. They smiled as they were frisked and checked with metal detectors on their way in. Military and police presence was heavy, and completely worthless. The men picked up their metal boxes, now full of popcorn, peanuts, soft drinks, and Sarin bombs attached to explosives, and headed out to their assigned sections. If they were afraid, they hid it well.

It was after 6 PM, and the temperature outside of the stadium was almost a hundred degrees. Inside the state-of-the art stadium, giant chillers and misters sprayed cool water vapor into the air keeping it closer to seventy for the fans and the players. Only in the Middle East would you find air-conditioning outdoors. It was a beautiful night for soccer.

The energy in the stadium was palpable, with tens of thousands of fans waving team banners and cheering. The stadium was sold out as expected for two premier teams. Television crews on elevated mobile platforms moved around the field, filming the game live in high definition and broadcasting it around the globe.

Abdul Aziz checked his watch from his seat in the lower level. He had worn traditional clothing and keffiyeh, and watched with loathing as young women in soccer shirts jumped around flaunting their bodies. Their boyfriends seemed oblivious to the shamelessness of their women, and some even laughed and appeared to enjoy seeing them showoff in public.

Abdul glanced around the stadium and saw his men moving around through the crowds. Any moment, Rasheed would be detonating the Sarin in Al Udeid.

He smiled and stood, scanning the huge crowd. 40,000 perhaps? 50? How many would be choking to death as their skin blistered and their bodies twitched in their last agonizing minutes? He headed for the exit, his hand wrapped around the cell phone in his pocket.

With the increase in security at Al Udeid, the concrete jersey barriers at the entrance roadways had been shifted from straight roadways to zigzagged paths that prevented vehicles from picking up too much speed. At the end of the zig-zag alley, two young Marines stood post behind some sandbags under a tarp to stay out of the brutal sun. In full combat gear, standing on asphalt in a hundred degree weather wasn't very enjoyable. Their platoon sergeant had been by an hour earlier delivering water and checking in on them. His parting words were spit out harshly, *"No unauthorized personnel or vehicles get past you, clear?"*

The pair responded in unison with, "Yes, Sergeant."

As soon as the sergeant's jeep took off, Jonathan, a country boy from rural Virginia and the platoon comedian, looked at his friend Jordan and barked, *"You clear?"* in his best Sergeant Rawlings voice. Jordan, a lance corporal, laughed and said, *"Crystal!"* in his best *Top Gun* impersonation.

They sat in the heat for another ten minutes, arguing over whether the Ford F-150 or Dodge Ram was the better pickup truck. Jonathan, a corporal, was due to head home in another month and was deciding on his new truck. He had been "showing Jordan the ropes" when Jordan's head swiveled to the road. "Yo, yo! D-Man! Vehicles coming down the road, way too fast, bro!" Jordan was a Long Islander, and his accent and expressions were a strong contrast to the country boy. He was a little younger than Jonathan at nineteen, but already had his pilot's license. He was a smart, detail-oriented kid who was rapidly becoming a favorite grunt to his platoon leaders.

The two of them immediately jumped up and got behind their two machine guns. On auto-pilot, the two corporals went safeties-off and leaned into their SAWs.

"They ain't slowing down," Jonathan shouted.

"Son of a bitch, there's four of 'em! This is the real deal! I'm sending a warning downrange!"

Jonathan grabbed his radio and reported back to base security. "Echo George to base! Unauthorized vehicles inbound!"

The thought of actually firing a few rounds at vehicles on base was almost as scary as the potential threat. What if they weren't bad guys attacking the base, but rather some VIPs coming in unannounced? Still—they were driving fast and erratically while the base was on high alert. They had over 10,000 brothers behind them, along with a few billion dollars in aircraft. There was no way anyone was getting past them as long as they were breathing. The three vehicles behind the lead SUV stopped. The SUV in front revved and picked up speed. It was now obvious that this was an attack—a suicide bomber, no doubt. They could run for cover and save themselves or do everything possible to stop the vehicles, no matter what. Their decision to stand and fight was instantaneous.

A short burst of heavy machinegun fire over the SUV did nothing to slow it down.

"Jordan! He's still coming!" Screamed Jonathan as he threw his radio and put his hand back on his weapon.

"Fuck this! Unload!" Shouted Jordan, his finger now squeezing controlled bursts at the cab of the lead vehicle, a dark SUV.

Jonathan began firing his weapon as well, aiming for the cab and engine block behind the grill. The SUV's driver floored it, swerving and side swiping the concrete barriers as he closed the distance on the guards.

Jonathan and Jordan were no longer speaking. The two young corporals focused every ounce of their being on stopping the lead vehicle. They knew how these attacks went down. They'd seen them before. They also knew they were the only thing between the attackers and the barracks behind them. They held their triggers down and sent hundreds of rounds into the SUV. The driver was hit several times and was dying, but not before he managed to push his foot to the floor and release the trigger mechanism in his hand.

Jordan's last seconds were spent watching his rounds impact the driver, thinking he had stopped the man in time. The flash of light ended the lives of the two young corporals instantly, sending the guardhouse and pieces of the barriers for hundreds of feet. Seventy yards behind the lead vehicle that had disappeared in the explosion, three cars now sped up through the zigzag path. Rasheed had seen Imad disappear and said a prayer for him. The amount of explosives had created a deep crater, and Rasheed now had to push through the wreckage and move past the barriers without falling into the smoking black hole. This was going to take much longer than he anticipated. He used his car to push the remaining wreckage out of his way and move around the remnants of the guardhouse while the two cars behind him also tried to maneuver around huge obstacles of burning wreckage and chunks of concrete and asphalt.

He was praying out loud, very quickly, without even realizing he was doing it. Sweat dripped off his face as he got past the wreckage and floored the gas pedal towards the buildings down the road. He checked his rearview mirror and saw the two cars trying to follow him.

"God is great," he repeated, gripping the wheel and driving as fast as his car would go.

CHAPTER 39

Al Udeid

Eric was walking Earl back to the infirmary for a quick bandage change and wound check. The previous meeting had frustrated the team members, who weren't used to sitting on the sidelines when there was something big going down.

"You saved my ass, E," said Earl from out of nowhere as they walked. His mind had been churning a hundred miles an hour since his conversation with Cascaes.

Eric didn't know what to say, so he said nothing. They continued walking.

"I froze, man," he said quietly.

"It was dark. You and the hajji almost walked into each other, man."

Earl stopped walking and looked at Eric. "I froze, plain and simple. We don't *hesitate*. We're trained to react instantly. I saw the guy's face...saw how young he was...I just stared at him."

Eric had stopped walking, too. "Look, man. I had your back. It's over. I know the ambush messed with your head. I was lucky—I didn't have to see it up close. But I put a round through the driver, and a second one through one of those kids. It's fucked up, Earl. But this is the sandbox. *Everything* out here is fucked up."

Earl looked down at his feet.

"You always talk about how bad your neighborhood was growing up. Did the kids in your neighborhood all walk around with AK47s chanting 'death to somebody' while their parents encouraged them? I don't think so. I've been in Iraq, A-Stan, and now here. For every kid I see that reminds me of the kids at home, I see another one that would ghost me in *two seconds*. You gotta stay frosty, man."

An explosion in the distance stopped Earl before he could respond. They both looked towards the direction of the explosion, looked back at each other, and then started sprinting towards their barracks where their weapons were stowed and the rest of the team was lounging.

"That's the east gate!" yelled Eric as they ran.

Earl ripped off the sling as he ran, whipping it to the ground as they sprinted. By the time they got to the barracks, some of the other men inside were starting to run out, most with weapons.

"East gate!" yelled Earl as he pushed past a few men and bounded up the stairs. Eric was right behind him. They made it to their wing of the building in less than three minutes, passing other Marines who were now heading outside. A few were on their phones, trying to reach their superiors.

Mackey and Cascaes were already coming out of the door with their weapons when Earl and Eric got there.

"East gate got hit!" yelled Eric as he raced to his weapons locker to retrieve his sniper rifle. Earl grabbed his M4 and stumbled out of the room into the hallway where the rest of the team was now racing towards the stairs as they snapped magazines into their weapons.

By the time they got downstairs, the base sirens were going off and they could hear gunfire.

"If they have Sarin we're fucked," screamed Mackey as he and Cascaes sprinted towards the noise. They were both in civilian clothes and carried M4 carbines. The air base was huge, but their barracks were only a short run from the gate.

A couple of Marines had hopped into trucks and were roaring off towards the sound of the explosion. Mackey and Cascaes ran in the street behind the truck, which quickly distanced itself from them. The rest of the team was catching up to the two Chrises, with Earl and Eric only a little behind. A Marine Cobra gunship roared over their heads towards the attack.

"That's it!" screamed Mackey to the assault copter. "Go!"

It had taken Rasheed almost six minutes to maneuver around the wreckage. He was driving through the base looking for the large barracks he had studied in the picture of the base that Abdul had given him; but now that he was actually driving, he was a little confused. There were buildings and tents and airplane hangars in every direction. To detonate at the wrong place would be a waste of his life. He needed to find the barracks or the mess hall and prayed that Allah would guide him to the enemy. Behind him, the other two drivers sped and swerved through the narrow streets. A few Marines and airmen ran out of the way of the vehicles as they realized something was wrong. Most of them weren't armed while walking around on base and could do nothing but run and try and call base security on their cell phones.

Rasheed came to a crossroads. He hesitated for a moment and looked around. A left turn—it was a left turn. As he began to accelerate, he heard it before he saw it. He looked up and saw what looked like a very small plane—no, not a plane, a helicopter. Rasheed pushed the gas pedal to the floor and cut his wheel left. He began praying loudly and racing towards where he thought the large barracks were.

The Cobra pilot pressed the trigger and unleashed a fifty round burst from his M197 .20 mm electric cannon. The lead car vibrated in a cloud of sand and dust as the rounds impacted the passenger compartment. With a quick flick of his thumb, the pilot fired a hellfire missile into the vehicle and watched it explode in a huge fireball.

⊕

The team was still racing towards the gate when they heard the explosion.

"Cobra got him!" screamed Mackey triumphantly.

"What about the Sarin?" screamed Cascaes as they ran.

"We have to warn everyone! They have to clear out of there!"

They turned the corner and saw the burning car at the end of a long road, maybe a half a mile away. A few Marines and MPs were ahead of them running towards the wreckage.

"Stay back! Stay back!" yelled Cascaes.

"Sarin! They're loaded with Sarin!" screamed Mackey. It was useless, the Cobra was firing its mini-gun at another vehicle that had taken off down a side road and was racing towards the rows of tents the Marines used as living quarters. The second car was being hit by the gunfire but kept speeding towards the tents. The third car swerved around the wreck of Rasheed's car and raced straight towards the team.

Eric dropped to a knee and pulled the caps off of his sniper rifle. He glanced quickly at the American flag hanging limp on the pole—no wind. Moving faster than normal, he chambered a round and put the scope to his eye. Everyone on the street with a weapon began firing at the car, but it was still too far away and moving erratically at high speed.

Eric looked through his scope and could see the face of the driver. He inhaled, exhaled, and put the crosshairs on the driver's face.

CHAPTER 40

Abdul Aziz pushed his way through the crowd and headed for the exit. There were uniformed police and soldiers with MP5s everywhere. He kept his Keffiyeh close to his face and avoided eye contact. When he reached the top of the stairs, he looked back out into the stadium. The match was in full-swing, and the crowd was loud and excited. Abdul began scanning for his men. He could see them mixed with the other hawkers all over the stadium. They were spread out for maximum damage. The world would not have seen an attack of this magnitude since 9-11. Abdul smiled and began quickly walking towards the escalator that would bring him outside. He would go to his car, dial the number that would detonate the boxes, and drive back to Saudi Arabia where he would assemble another group of followers for the next attack.

Hodges was on one knee, blocking out the chaos around him. All he heard was his own heartbeat and breathing, which he was trying to control. He exhaled, inhaled, held his breath, and ever so slowly squeezed the trigger as he held the drivers face in his cross-hairs. The car was less than a half-mile away and headed straight towards them.

The rifle let out a loud blast, recoiled slightly, and then Hodges held it steady, staring through the scope again. The man's face had exploded inside the spider-webbed windshield, and the car veered sharply to its right where it struck a concrete barrier and stopped. Eric was sure the driver was dead, but with a possible finger on a trigger, he was taking no chances. He fired a second round that removed a good portion of the man's head, and then put three rounds into the engine block to make sure the car wouldn't move again.

The other members of the team were still running towards the gunfire when the Cobra fired off another missile. It struck the last remaining vehicle, which exploded and flipped on to its roof. The gunship fired several mini-gun bursts, and the car began burning.

Cascaes yelled to Mackey. "What about the Sarin?"

"We just have to keep everyone clear. There's no breeze and the fire will help destroy the chemical. Tell the team— keep everyone back!" Mackey handed Cascaes his encrypted satellite phone and began running towards a jeep.

"Where are you going?" asked Cascaes.

"Airfield!" he screamed back, never breaking stride. "Call Dex and have him call this base! I need emergency authorization to run an op *now*!"

Cascaes ran to Moose and Ripper who were standing nearby watching the vehicles burn in stunned silence. "We need to keep everyone back! Spread the team out and tell everyone it's Sarin. They need to keep away and get EOD over to the car Hodges took out. It can still go off. *Go!*" As soon as the team moved into action, Cascaes hit redial and called Dex Murphy in Langley.

Moose relayed the orders to the team and the men began racing through the streets screaming at everyone they saw to stay back because of the Sarin. It didn't take much convincing— when the word Sarin was heard, everyone began hustling away from the wreckage. Everyone, that is, except for a Marine sergeant who raced past Moose towards the destroyed gate.

"Hey!" Yelled Moose. "You hear me? That's Sarin gas! Stop!"

The sergeant ignored him and kept running. Moose and Ripper hauled ass after him. *"Hey! Stop!"*

The sergeant was heading for the two men at the front gate—his two corporals he had posted a few hours earlier. He heard Moose and Ripper yelling at him to stop, but ran as fast as he could anyway. He was getting close to the vehicle that Hodges had stopped when Moose tackled his legs and took him down.

"What the fuck?" screamed the surprised Marine.

"I said *stop*! There's Sarin gas all over the place!"

"I've got two men at the gate!" screamed the sergeant.

"They're *dead*!" yelled Moose. "And if you get any closer, you'll be dead, too! It's too late!"

The sergeant struggled to get up, but Moose was too strong. Moose ended up giving the stranger a bear hug and saying, "I'm sorry, Sergeant. They're gone, brother." The stranger began sobbing, and Moose just sat on the ground with him holding him close.

CHAPTER 41

Mackey had driven like a lunatic to the airstrip while screaming into his radio to the control tower.

"I need a Prowler on the runway immediately!" he was screaming at the tower controller. "Get me the fucking General or whoever you need to authorize it *now!*"

The major on the phone didn't know Mackey from a hole in the wall, but he also knew the base was under attack. He patched Mackey through to the flight coordinator, a Lieutenant Colonel Forrest, who had just received a call from General Houston, the base commander. By the time the lieutenant colonel agreed to supply the Prowler, Mackey was already at the runway where the four crewmen from the Marine Tactical Electronic Warfare Squadron 3, the "Moon Dogs" were scrambling to their jet.

"Who's the copilot?" screamed Mackey.

"Me," answered a captain.

"Not today! I'm going up with these guys and I can fly."

"No fucking way. Who the hell are you?"

"I'm CIA, authorized by the President of the United States—you got any problems, you take it up with him. You the pilot?" he screamed at one of the men. That man looked at another captain who said he was.

"Let's go! We need to be wheels up now! I'll explain in the air! We've got to stop another attack!" He was still holding his assault rifle.

"Look, I'm not a regular copilot!" screamed the first captain. "I'm an electronics counter measures officer! I'm responsible for defending this aircraft."

"This aircraft doesn't need defending, and this is a short hop. We have a simple mission and we're out of here. We need to move *now*!" He pointed the rifle at the captain.

The crew didn't like it, but they also knew they weren't witnessing a normal day. They ran towards the waiting jet and began climbing the ladder to the cockpit. The pilot dropped into his seat and called the flight commander in the tower.

"Sir, I've got some lunatic telling me he's authorized to fly with me and direct this aircraft! What am I supposed to do?"

"Go! The base is under attack, and I've got authorization from the Joint Chiefs. That guy with you is a spook, but he's a pilot. Do whatever he says, that's right from the top. You're cleared for takeoff!"

The flight team strapped in and began closing the cockpit while the flight crew on the ground watched the whole bizarre scene in amazement.

"Head to the soccer stadium!" Mackey screamed at the pilot.

"You're not in a flight suit. If I go full speed, you're going to pass out."

"I'll be fine, you're under one G. Haul ass, Captain!"

The pilot had been cleared for takeoff. He radioed the tower and asked for a heading for the soccer stadium. As soon as the crew was ready and the ground crew gave a quick salute, the pilot threw the plane to take off speed and they roared down the runway. Mackey could feel his eyeballs trying to go through the back of his head and grimaced as the jet headed up at top speed. They banked and flew at over 500 miles an hour towards the stadium.

"What's the deal?" asked the pilot.

As soon as Mackey's head cleared, he said, "Terrorists may be planning to hit the stadium like they did here. If they're using remote detonators, you need to jam the stadium."

"Roger that. You copy, Two and Three?"

The Electronics Counter Measures Officers in the rear, ECMO2 and 3, responded. "Copy, Skipper. Jamming the stadium."

The jet roared over the desert making a beeline for the stadium. It was, as Mackey promised, a very quick trip at 500 knots.

"There's the stadium, ten o'clock," said the pilot, who slowed and banked to begin a holding flight pattern above the stadium below.

The ECMOs in the rear began their electronic attack. Every cell phone call below immediately ended, and a myriad of other electronic problems began. The announcer inside the soccer stadium lost his microphone, the large replay screens went static, the remote controlled thermostats on the massive chillers ceased operation, and the hundreds of flatscreen TVs placed around the stadium in bathrooms and eateries went black.

⊕

Abdul Aziz sat in his car. He prayed and thanked Allah, then pulled the phone from his pocket. Scanning around him for security personnel and seeing no one nearby, Abdul dialed the number that would detonate the eighty Sarin bombs all over the stadium.

"*Allahu Akbar!*" shouted Abdul as he pressed the Send button.

He listened and waited.

Nothing happened. Abdul waited another second, and then he realized he was much too far away to hear the explosions. They were only small charges designed to vaporize the Sarin and send the clouds of gas into the crowds.

He nodded. He wouldn't get to enjoy hearing the explosions or screaming yet. That wouldn't be until he was safely at a place that had a television camera. He waited another few seconds.

Wait.

If the Sarin went off inside the stadium, there would be hundreds of panicked soccer fans streaming from the exits. Something was wrong. Abdul drove his car down the long aisle of cars and headed closer to the stadium. He could see police officers and soldiers walking calmly outside. Did they not know that the bombs had gone off yet? Was everyone dead inside? Was that possible?

Abdul drove all the way to the first row of parking, nearest the stadium, and stopped. He opened his car door and stepped out into the hot sun. He could hear normal cheering inside the stadium. Something was wrong. Abdul pointed his phone at the stadium and pressed Send again. Nothing.

He could feel panic inside his chest. Abdul got back into his car and roared out of the parking lot to the highway that would take him back to Saudi Arabia. If his attack had been foiled, then what about the base? He drove as fast as his car would go once he cleared the stadium roads. On the highway, he was driving almost a hundred miles an hour when he decided to try Rasheed's phone. He was now ten miles from the stadium and beyond the range of the Prowler that was, unknown to him, jamming the stadium. He called Rasheed's number and it went immediately to voice mail. It was most likely good news—their attack had already occurred. He would make sure. He called other numbers of the group to see if they would be answered.

⊕

The EOD squad was wearing gas masks along with their regular extra heavy bomb- resistant Kevlar and ceramic plates. They had carefully opened the doors of the vehicle and were looking for detonators and trigger devices. The driver was very dead, with his head blown all over the inside of the car. One of the EODs, who had opened the passenger door, had just spotted the detonator near the driver's hand when a cell phone rang. The two EODs inside the car closed their eyes and waited to die.

It rang again. And a third time.

"What the fuck?" asked the nervous EOD.

The Senior EOD1, who was hunched over the driver, stared with wide eyes at the phone. "I think the hajji's getting a regular phone call." He laughed nervously.

The other EOD, sweat running down his legs and into his boots, said, "I'm sorry, Hajji can't come to the phone right now. His head's blown off. Please leave your name and number, and he'll call you from Hell."

"Take the phone. Give it to the Major. G2s gonna want to take a look."

The EOD gingerly took the phone and stepped back from the car. He held it up and showed another EOD, who quickly moved forward and took it from him. "It's not a detonator. It just rang."

The EOD took the phone and jogged it back to the lieutenant who was overseeing the explosives ordnance disposal team. Cascaes was nearby and saw the exchange. He jogged over to the lieutenant.

"Excuse me, Lieutenant. I'm Special Operations, I need to see that phone," said Cascaes.

The lieutenant looked at the stranger in civilian clothes like he had three heads. "Back up, son, we're in the middle of trying to take a bomb apart."

"I need the phone. The Director of the CIA and the Chairman of the Joint Chiefs know I'm here, and I need that phone. I'm Senior Chief Chris Cascaes. You tell him that. Now, you can hand it to me, or I can shoot you." He was glaring at the lieutenant, and although he wasn't pointing his weapon, it was in his hands. "Call whoever you need to call, and hand me the god damned phone, lieutenant."

The lieutenant face was red with anger. He handed the phone to Cascaes and pulled his radio off his belt to call the base commander. Cascaes didn't stick around to listen. He jogged back to his team, who had reassembled to watch the EOD team work on the car that Hodges had stopped.

Cascaes pulled up the recent calls on the phone and then used his own phone to call Dex Murphy who picked it up immediately.

"Dex, I'm going to read off a phone number. It was an incoming number to a cell phone we just took off a dead bomber at the base. Maybe you can get a GPS on the phone."

"Outstanding, read it to me."

Cascaes gave Dex the number, and Dex hung up and started making phone calls.

CHAPTER 42

It had been a frantic few minutes of calls between Langley, Cascaes, base commanders, and flight crews. When it was settled, Cascaes grabbed Moose and relayed the latest orders.

"Here's the deal. Whoever called the bomber that Hodges took out is heading out of the area on Route 5. We have his cell phone GPS. I want you to grab a couple of men and hop a Black Hawk to that location. We want him alive, Moose. You bring his ass back here and we find them all. You copy?"

"Roger that, Skipper. I'll take Ripper and Hodges. I'll bring him back."

"Alive, Moose!"

"Yes, sir," he snapped, and then ran off to tell Ripper and Hodges.

☩

Abdul was racing down the desert highway towards the border. With the base attack successful, border security might be tougher. His passport was forged, and his alias wouldn't raise any suspicion, but still he was worried. He turned on the car radio and listened to Al Jazeera, hoping to hear news of the attacks. It was regular programming. Abdul cursed under his breath.

Why hadn't the Sarin bombs gone off? They had tested the prototypes and they had worked every time. What had gone wrong?

✛

High overhead, thirty miles away, an EA-6B Prowler circled the airspace over the stadium, jamming all frequencies. The pilot received an incoming transmission from the airbase.

"Big Dog, this is Downtown. I have a message for your second seat, over."

The pilot looked over at Mackey in the second seat.

"Downtown, second seat is ears on, go ahead with your message, over."

Mackey listened intently.

"Just took a call from the Virginia Company. A cell phone recovered by EOD gave a number and GPS location of a target. There's a small team en route to intercept. Security at the stadium has been alerted and the rest of the team is en route. Continue all electronic countermeasures. Over."

The pilot looked at Mackey. "That mean something to you? We're supposed to stay here on station."

"Yeah. Listen, the same group that attacked Al Udeid tried to hit the stadium. If our guys grabbed a phone off a dead bomber, it means they may be able to trace it back to the caller. But the stadium still has whatever Sarin bomb they hid in there. You just keeping jamming everything. My team is heading over to help the locals."

The team had been ordered by Dex to head over to the stadium. With the base threat resolved, and the stadium attack imminent, the Joint Chiefs had convinced the President to send in the team. Three of the base EODs were still working on the last car bomb, but there were three others on the base and two of them had bomb dogs.

An EA-6B Prowler and a Black Hawk helicopter roared off after the GPS coordinates gleaned from the phone number. As long as the phone stayed on, the Prowler and Black Hawk would find it. In the rear of the helicopter, Moose, Ripper, and

Hodges rechecked weapons and discussed how they would take down the car without killing the occupant.

The rest of the team, now accompanied by the two EODs with their K9 partners, were in a Blackhawk helicopter roaring over the desert towards the stadium.

"Who are you guys?" asked the Senior EOD, a dog handler named Mark Franklin.

Cascaes played it as straight as he could. "Senior Chief Chris Cascaes. We're Special Operations and we were never here, you copy? We need you and your dogs. All you need to know is that we're good at what we do, and we need *you* to be good at what you do."

Franklin nodded and extended a hand. "Mark Franklin, and that's Jeff Krekeler. Our K9s are the best. If there's a bomb in the stadium, we'll find it. The only problem is, it's a big stadium, and there's only two of us. What are we looking for? Any idea?"

"That's the problem. We don't know. We have a Prowler from the base running countermeasures. If it's an electronic detonator, we're safe. If there's someone inside holding a trigger, we're fucked. We're assuming it's a bomb to detonate Sarin gas into the crowd. That means dispersal. The stadium is climate controlled, so maybe we check around the chillers first. Getting it into the air vents is a good way to get it into the air. Other than that, I don't have any good guesses. The stuff works best when detonated from above and allowed to rain down like a mist. I think we start the search from the top of the stadium at the chillers and work our way down."

"Roger that. Damn. Sarin? Are they evacuating the stadium?" asked Franklin.

"Negative. We still don't have one hundred percent proof the attack is even going down here, and even if we did—if we start evacuating, maybe they detonate as soon as they realize we're on to them. We need to find the bomb and kill the bomber. Oh, and try and hold your breath if things go south."

"That's great, thanks."

The Black Hawk banked hard and the pilot's voice came over the speakers. "Time to LZ sixty seconds."

Jon yelled over to Cascaes inside the loud aircraft. "Hey, Skipper, the security at the stadium know we're inbound?"

"I sure hope so. The last thing we need is the good guys shooting at us."

CHAPTER 43

Abdul Aziz called ahead to a safe house in Saudi Arabia outside of Riyadh where other members of the New Wahhabi Jihad were staying. He notified his contact that he would be there before sunup and asked if there was any news about the American airbase or the soccer game in Qatar. His contact, a man named Rafika, told him that the American airbase had been attacked, and two American Marines had been killed, but that was all he had heard. The would-be bombers had all been killed. When Abdul heard that, his face turned purple with rage.

"Two? *Two* Americans? They're lying! They're covering up the truth! There must be hundreds—*thousands* dead!" He was screaming into the phone.

"I don't know," said Rafika, fear in his voice.

⊕

High overhead, the ECM officer in the rear of the Prowler spoke to the pilot. "Captain, I have confirmation on that GPS coordinate. There's a phone call in progress. Looks like the target is still on Highway 5 headed for the border. Time to target two minutes."

"Roger that, I'll notify Hunter One. Light up the target."

The ECM officer pressed a few buttons and pinpointed the target vehicle with laser guidance. "Target is painted."

"Hunter One, this is Moon Dog Five. We have painted your target. Highway 5, heading southwest. Over."

"Roger, Moon Dog Five. We have the target. Acquiring visual, over."

Abdul continued his rant in the car as he drove. It wasn't Rafika's fault the news hadn't been made public yet, but he flinched with every curse and insult that Abdul shouted.

"Moon Dog Five, we have visual confirmation at this time. Vehicle is driving southeast on Highway 5. Looks like one occupant. Over."

"Roger, Hunter One. We're jamming and his cell phone won't function. Take down the target."

"Roger, Moon Dog Five. Time to target, twenty seconds."

Rafika tried his best to calm Abdul. "The Americans are just embarrassed, Abdul. The truth will come out soon. Hello? Abdul?" The phone had gone dead, compliments of the Moon Dog overhead.

Abdul was still screaming at Rafika when his phone stopped working.

The crew chief was listening to his pilot, and yelled over to Moose, Ripper, and Hodges. "Okay, boys—we're here. Target is the silver Mercedes below. There's not another car for miles. How do you want to do this?"

Moose yelled back, "Ask the pilot to move us out to the side a bit and pull even with the car. Our sniper is going to stop the engine, and when I tell you, I need your pilot to put us down right over the car. We're going to rope out, grab this hajji, and get right back on the bird. Then we haul ass back to base."

The crew chief explained back to the pilot, who banked right and increased speed to pull into a blind spot over the car below. The helicopter pilot kept their position steady, and Ripper slid the side door open. Hodges leaned against the door frame with his sniper rifle.

"That's it. Keep holding steady," the crew chief told the pilot.

They hovered.

A single loud gunshot echoed through the aircraft, and the .338 Lapua round blasted through the engine block. Hodges chambered another round and hit it again. Smoke billowed from the engine, and the car rapidly slowed down.

Inside the car, it took Abdul a moment to realize what had happened. First, his cell phone had stopped working, and then a loud *BANG* and his car was shuddering. Now, a second loud explosion and his engine was steaming and smoking as his dashboard lights all came on. He lost his steering and fought hard against the car, pulling it to the side of the road.

By the time Abdul's car came to a full stop, a giant black helicopter blocked out his view of everything through his windshield. Abdul was horrified. What was happening? As his brain tried to catch up with impossible events, two giant human beings dropped to the ground from ropes that appeared on both sides of his smoldering car. He stared in disbelief at the man next to his window as the window on the passenger side exploded.

Ripper use the butt of his assault rifle to smash the window and reach in to open the door. Moose held his assault rifle pointed right at Abdul's terrified face. Ripper hit the unlock button on his now-open door, and as soon as Moose heard

it click, he pulled the driver-side door open and slammed
his hand into Abdul's throat. Abdul's eyes went very wide
as he choked and lost his breath. Before he knew what was
happening, Moose had pulled him out of the car, facedown
on the blistering hot asphalt. Ripper hopped over the smoking
hood and dropped down next to them, pulling plastic zip-ties,
which he used to secure Abdul's wrists behind his back. They
pulled the gasping man to his feet and dragged him quickly
to the Black Hawk, which had spun around and landed on the
road for their exit. They pushed Abdul inside, where Hodges
slammed him against the metal floor. Ripper hopped up and sat
on him as Moose jumped in and pulled the door closed behind.
The crew chief told the pilot they were ready, and the bird
tilted forward and lifted off the ground, banking hard towards
the base.

Moose photographed the stunned Abdul Aziz while Ripper
scanned his fingerprints. Before they had travelled five miles,
Abdul Aziz's information had been sent to Dex Murphy in
Langley.

Moose radioed Cascaes, "Package is safe and secure.
Heading back to base, out."

A lone silver Mercedes sat smoking on the empty highway.

CHAPTER 44

Stadium

The Black Hawk touched down outside the stadium in the parking lot and the team jumped out, the dogs trotting alongside their handlers. Two Qatari Army soldiers watched in shock as the team jogged towards them. They looked to each other for guidance, but had no idea what to do.

Cascaes screamed at the two men as they ran towards them. "You speak English?"

One of the men nodded. "Little," he said in a heavy accent.

Cascaes cursed under his breath. "Bomb! You understand?"

The man looked at him blankly.

"Ka-Boom!" screamed Cascaes, pointing at the stadium, and then at the dogs. "Dogs look for Ka-Boom!"

The two men shouted back and forth in Arabic for a few seconds. They then began running towards the stadium, motioning the team to follow them. The group sprinted to the entrance, the Qatari men screaming at everyone they saw until one soldier finally ran to Cascaes. "I speak English. What's going on?"

Cascaes looked at the man's uniform. He appeared to be some kind of officer. "We have intelligence that there may be a bomb inside, armed with Sarin gas. We need to get to the chillers upstairs." The officer yelled back in Arabic for the two men to bring the team upstairs. They raced off to the escalators, the officer watching them go. As soon as they were out of sight,

169

he began walking quickly out of the stadium. Whatever he was being paid wasn't enough to be blown up with a Sarin bomb.

The team ran up the escalator to the first level and then again to the second level. Cascaes looked around for the officer, but he was nowhere to be found. Cascaes did his best to explain that he was looking for the air-conditioning system, but was getting nowhere. EOD Franklin spoke up. "Hey! Tucker's got something!" The large black shepherd was sniffing the air and the ground. He was obviously getting the scent of something.

"Work, Tucker! Work!" yelled Franklin.

The dog began pulling him inside the stadium and the other dog began whining. The other handler spoke to his partner as well. "Good boy, Cody. Get to work."

Both handlers followed their dogs into the stadium where tens of thousands of fans were screaming as Manchester United kicked a goal into the top right corner of the net. The fans were on their feet as the team entered the top of the second tier of seats. The dogs pulled at their leashes and the handlers spoke to each other.

"I'm taking him off lead. Work, Tucker!" he commanded as he unsnapped the leash from the dog's collar. The other handler did the same thing, and the two large dogs ran down the steps towards a food vendor. Fans on the aisle seats who saw the dogs running down the stairs spun around to see where they came from. They were even more surprised to see commandos with assault rifles coming down behind the dogs.

The dogs raced to the food vendor and stopped, barking at the man's food container.

"You gotta be shittin' me," said Moose. "Dog wants a hotdog?"

The food vendors turned white when he saw the dogs. He dropped the box and began fighting his way through the seats to exit the other side of the section. Moose saw him and yelled behind him to the team members coming down the stairs. He pointed to the other aisle and screamed, "Go around the other side!"

Four of the men turned and ran back up the stairs to head him off on the other side. The dogs sat and stared at the box, ignoring the nuts and dried fruit that had spilled all over the stairs. They were totally focused on the aluminum box.

"Good find!" said Franklin, as he knelt down and patted his dog's shoulder. He looked up at Cascaes, who was now standing over him. "What do you want me to do? I can look inside it here, but we need to get these people out of here."

"No, let's get it out of here," said Cascaes. The EOD picked up the box carefully and began walking up the stairs with it, the dogs close behind. The fans were now watching closely, and began asking questions. They were told to remain calm, and stay where they were.

As soon as the team had gotten to the top of the stairs with the box, they quickly moved away from the crowd to an outside area farther away that overlooked the parking lot. The dogs both began sniffing the air again and pacing around nervously.

"Shit," said Franklin.

"What?" asked Cascaes.

"They ain't done."

The other EOD opened the top of the box and looked inside. He gently removed whatever snacks were inside until it was empty. He stared at it for a second confused, and then realized what he was looking at. "False bottom," he announced.

"Okay, everyone move away. We need to take the bottom off; it may be booby-trapped," said Franklin.

"What about you?" asked Cascaes.

"It's what we do. Move away."

Cascaes motioned with his chin to head over the section where four of his guys were still trying to grab the food vendor. A few went down the same aisle again in case the guy had doubled back, and the rest headed to the other side of that section.

Franklin dropped his pack of tools and began slowly disassembling the bottom of the box. "Tommy, I'm opening the cover."

The two of them held their breath as Mark slowly lifted the aluminum plate. Beneath it was a Sarin bomblet wrapped in cushioning, attached to a cell phone that was lit up and waiting for a call.

"Bingo," he said calmly. Mark calmly pulled the wire lead from the phone, removed the phone from the box, and turned it off. He looked up at Jeff Krekeler. "Tucker and Cody think there's more."

"Yeah. Now what?"

Mark studied the bomb. "If they're all like this, they're all waiting for a call. As long as the Prowler's flying, we should be cool. The only way to detonate this manually is to take it apart, unwrap the bomblet, and break it open."

"Yeah, but how many more are inside?"

Mark shook his head. This was bad.

He stood up and looked over at Cascaes who was standing close enough to have been killed anyway. "Hey, Chief, I got good news and bad news." He explained what was going on.

Cascaes thought for a minute before speaking. "I've got an idea, but we're going to need a lot of help and someone who speaks better Arabic than me."

A young blonde woman appeared out of the stadium and saw Cascaes and the K9 units. She asked the two Qatari soldiers in Arabic what was going on. As soon as Cascaes heard her speak, he jogged over to her.

"Hey! You!"

The woman stopped in mid sentence and stared at him. "What's going on?" she demanded.

"You're American?"

"I asked you what's going on. Should this place be evacuated?"

"Look, lady, I need your help. You speak fluent Arabic?"

She put her hands on her hips and stared as Cascaes. "Did I stutter? I asked you a question!"

"There may be bombs inside this stadium. We can*not* allow the crowd to panic, you understand? If the bombers know we're on to them, they can detonate poison gas. I need your help—your language skills!"

The woman, named Patty, worked for an American oil and gas company in Qatar, and lived and worked in Doha. She spoke fluent Arabic. She took a deep breath and tried to be calm. "What is it that you need me to do?"

Cascaes looked at his watch. It was quarter to eight. "Look, I need for you to explain to these guys that they have to radio every cop and soldier in this stadium and instruct them to locate all the food vendors. We have no idea how many other bombs there are, but there may be a lot. I think they're using the food vendors to scatter the stuff around the crowd. They need to move casually to wherever these vendors are and get fairly close. At exactly eight o'clock, they're to grab these guys and make them put down the boxes. Exactly eight o'clock, okay? We have to try and get these guys all at once. If they realize they're being grabbed, they may be able to detonate these things in the crowd. You understand?"

The woman's face had gone from a healthy tan to corpse-white. "Oh, my God," she whispered.

"Focus! Listen, I need you to help me. Explain everything I said nice and simple to this soldier."

She nodded, worrying about her husband inside the stadium with their friends. There were almost 50,000 people inside. Her mind was racing and she felt sick.

Chris grabbed her arm and gently moved her closer to the Qatari soldiers. Patty began explaining, in a slow calm voice, even though she was sweating. The soldiers nodded and listened, and the n spoke rapidly to each other and then back to her. Patty looked at Chris and said, "They said it's impossible; there's hundreds of food vendors all over the stadium."

"It's not impossible. There are thousands of troops and cops all over this stadium. We just need to locate the vendors walking around with these boxes. Tell him he has to do it."

They argued back and forth a little bit and, finally, one of the soldiers began speaking into his radio. It was dead.

"Son of a bitch. The Moon Dogs are jamming all the frequencies," said Chris. "This won't work."

As Chris stood feeling helpless, Ernie P. ran over. "Hey, Skipper, we got the hajji that tried to run."

Cascaes looked at the woman. "What's your name?" he asked.

"Patty."

"I need you to help again with your Arabic. Come on."

They ran over to the other side of the section, where Jon and Raul were holding the bomber. "Ask him how many bombs there are in the stadium."

Patty spoke to him in Arabic. He spit at her, but missed. Chris responded with a knee directly into the man's groin. If not for Jon and Raul holding him by his arms, he would have hit the deck. Cascaes smacked his face a couple of times and then held his gun against the man's forehead.

"Ask him again," he said to Patty.

She asked, but the man was praying and preparing to be shot. "He's not going to tell us anything," said Patty.

Cascaes grabbed the man by the throat and walked him to the Qatari soldiers. "Here," he grunted, and shoved the man towards them. The Qatari soldier held him at gunpoint. The members of the team began assembling near Cascaes, and he called them in closer.

"Fellas, it's just us. The Qatari radios won't work with jammers working, and we can't tell them to turn them off because of the bombs, so that's it. It's just us. We need to go through the stadium, one section at a time, and inconspicuously take the vendor boxes."

The American woman was listening from nearby. She walked over to the group. "I can spread the word to the other Qatari police."

Chris thought about it. He nodded. "Okay. That helps. Just explain to them they have to be subtle. No shooting. Just quietly get the vendor or the box out of the crowd."

"Can I get my husband and two friends to help? We all speak fluent Arabic."

"Go. And thanks, Patty."

She ran off towards her seats in the deafening stadium.

"Okay, this is it. One section at a time. Let's try to live to the end of the day, boys. 50,000 people are counting on us not to fuck this up. No pressure. Half of you with me clockwise, other half works around the other direction. See you on the other side of the stadium."

"What do we do with the boxes when we get them?" asked Jon.

"Bring them up the stairs and just put them in stacks against the walls. Grab Qatari cops or soldiers and just have them watch over them. If the bombers can't detonate by phone, they have to take them apart by hand and break the Sarin bomblets. If they try that, we'll probably see them."

"And we catch them trying, we cleared to fire?" asked Pete.

"Yes, but only if you have to. And for Christ sake don't hit any civilians. Now go!"

The team broke in half, and Cascaes took off with Lance, Jake, Raul, Ernie P., and Smitty. Cory, Ryan, Jon, Pete, and Ray headed off in the other direction. Each team took a K9 unit with them.

CHAPTER 45

Stadium, Upper Deck

One section at a time, the team moved through the crowd. The first two food vendors that Chris approached were clueless, and gave up their boxes, which were hustled up the stairs of the section, outside to the open hallway. The K9 unit sniffed around and didn't get a hit, so they continued. The third vendor saw them and tried to get away, but he couldn't get through the cheering crowd. Two of the men grabbed him and escorted him to the top of the stairs, where the dog confirmed the bomb. The man's wrists were zip-tied behind his back, and he was given to the Police officers who were now starting to get the word from Patty and her group.

"This is going to take too long," said Ernie P. to Chris as they ran to the next section.

"As long as the signals can't get to the triggers, we'll be okay. Just keep your eyes peeled. We miss one box, and it'll be thousands of casualties in a crowd like this."

On the other side of the stadium, the K9 unit pulled hard against his leash. "Work, Cody! Work!" commanded Jeff. The dog froze and eyed a food vendor who spotted the team and the K9 unit up in the hallway area outside the stadium seats. Cody sniffed at the air and barked. The food vendor looked terrified. He dropped to one knee and reached into the box, trying to pull the bottom off and get to the Sarin bomblet.

Jon aimed his M4, the red dot on the bomber's forehead, and fired a single silenced round. The man slumped over the box, dead instantly. Inside the stadium, the cheering crowd never heard the gunshot.

Ryan yelled, "I'll double-check this section. You guys take the next one and I'll catch up." The other five men took off to the next section with Cody, and Ryan sprinted down the aisle steps scanning for food vendors. There section was clear, so he ran back up. For most humans, sprinting up and down stadium steps might have been brutal. For the members of the team, it was just another day at the office.

Patty and her group had split up and were finding police officers and Qatari soldiers, relaying what was happening as fast as they could. She also explained, as Chris had explained to her, why no one's radio was working—the Americans were jamming the signals to prevent the bombs from being detonated. That seemed to backup her story, and even the most reluctant policemen began searching for the food vendors.

Twenty minutes later, there were sixty-three Qatari police and soldiers helping the team track down food vendors. And while there were numerous scuffles, tackles, fist fights, and foot chases, only three other bombers were killed with gunfire. Fortunately, the soccer match was so intense that the crowd was screaming wildly at the game and was oblivious for the most part. Seeing security grab people and drag them away wasn't note-worthy at a Man U – Spain game. By the time the team was reunited at the other end of the stadium, they had secured seventy-one rigged vendor boxes. The men were slightly winded and soaked with sweat.

Cascaes wiped his face with the back of his hand. "Okay, upper level is clear. I have Qatari cops stationed at the four corner escalators looking for any vendors that might try and come up from downstairs. Time for us to head down and do this all over again on the first level. We've got a lot more help now—it should go faster, but the game's almost over. These

bombers have to be wondering what's going on. They gotta
know something's up. They get desperate, they may try and
just cook them off manually, so move fast and shoot if you
have to. Move out!"

CHAPTER 46

Stadium, Lower Deck

The team was running down the escalator with dozens of police and soldiers running after them. Patty and her people had gotten the word out, and they were still bravely running all over the stadium finding help. Upstairs, dozens of would-be bombers were zip tied and held in the security offices, with soldiers stationed at vendor boxes awaiting disposal instructions.

Cascaes reached the bottom of the escalator and ran to the first section. He stuck his head in to see the remaining game time. Less than fifteen minutes.

Almost impossible to find them all, even with all the extra help.

And then a change in luck.

Tucker began whining, and EOD Franklin let him run. Cascaes and his men ran after the dog, who was the most excited he'd been since he'd started working. They ran around the bend in the wall at the far end of the stadium and found themselves looking at double doors that led to the vending area. The dogs were barking and straining to get through the doors. Chris and the team sprinted to the doors and opened them up, finding themselves staring down into the eyes of a dozen bombers, all of them on their knees working feverishly to take apart their vendor boxes.

Earlier, the bombers had realized something was wrong and had started finding each other, looking for some type of guidance. Eventually, one of the men suggested they detonate the bombs manually, but that meant taking the boxes apart and pulling out the bomblets. They couldn't do that inside the stadium with the crowd watching, so they had decided to go to the small room were the boxes had originally been stored to pull apart the metal. The team ran right into them.

"Freeze! Nobody move!" yelled Cascaes as he realized what he had stumbled upon. The dogs were barking wildly, but now they sat down and stared.

One of the bombers pulled his box apart and managed to get the bomblet out and separated from its cushion. He stood and cocked his arm to throw it. Three two-round bursts from three different weapons hit the man in the face and chest. He dropped the bomblet with a loud *pop* as the glass broke.

CHAPTER 47

Al Udeid

Dex was on the phone with Moose. "The guy you grabbed is Abdul Aziz, the leader of the New Wahhabi Jihad! You hit the jackpot, Moose!"

"Good news. Any word from the Skipper yet?" he asked. He was worried and hated being away from his guys when there was trouble.

"Not yet. Mackey is still in the air jamming the stadium. The team is on site, but we don't have any word from them, and we won't as long as the Prowler is jamming signals. We just have to wait. In the meantime, that phone you pulled off of Aziz has plenty of numbers. He called someone in Riyadh. As soon as the team gets back, you're taking down that address."

"You're pretty optimistic, considering there's some giant poison gas bomb in the soccer stadium, and we haven't heard from our people in hours," exclaimed Moose, obviously agitated.

"Moose, you know how good your team is. If there had been any type of explosion, we'd have heard about it by now. Just sit tight and wait."

"This Aziz guy wouldn't tell me shit."

"And he won't. Leave the interrogation to the professionals. We have methods for these things. You did your job."

Moose made a face. "Yeah, but if I could get this piece of shit to talk, maybe we could help our team."

"I understand your position, and I'm sure the urge to kick his teeth in is overwhelming. But he won't talk just because you smack him around a little."

"Who said it would be a *little*?" asked Moose.

"You're to stand down and await further instructions. That's a direct order. He's in a secure area?"

"Yeah, the brig, with two guards posted watching him."

"Perfect. He can't kill himself, and you can't kill him, either. My people will take him apart at the appropriate time. You completed an important assignment, Moose. This wasn't just some two-bit bad guy—this was the guy trying to wipe out an entire soccer stadium full of civilians and an American airbase. It was a huge catch. I'll be in touch." He hung up.

Ripper sat across the table with Hodges.

"So now what?" asked Ripper.

"We wait. I don't like it any more than you do. But we have to just wait."

Moose and Ripper spent the next twenty minutes staring at the phone, pacing around the small office like caged animals. When they couldn't take it anymore, they pulled their duffle bags and began cleaning weapons, sharpening combat knives, and changing batteries on night vision equipment—anything to stay busy, and be prepared for a call they prayed would come swiftly.

CHAPTER 48

Stadium

The shots echoed through the hallway and prep room, and everyone froze as the bomber dropped his bomblet of Sarin. When it hit the concrete floor, the glass *pop* was audible. For a split second, time stood still. A dozen bombers...a dozen Special Operators...just stared at the round glass bomblet as it lay broken and hissing on the floor. Upon contact with the air, the clear liquid foamed and vaporized, expanding quickly as it fogged the room.

In the next split second, Cascaes sprinted forward and slammed the doors shut. Realizing what Cascaes was doing, Jon raced forward and slammed against the doors as well. The rest of the team members joined them and, as they held the doors closed, the bombers inside began screaming and pushing from the other side. The tug of war on the double doors lasted for maybe thirty seconds, and the agonized screaming inside was horrific. The noise died down, leaving the team holding the doors closed against very weak pushing. They could hear coughing and gagging inside for another few seconds, and then the pushing against the door stopped altogether.

"Everyone back!" screamed Cascaes, afraid that the mist might start to leak out from under the doors.

The team pulled back and took up firing positions in case anyone made it out of the room. There were a few more coughs and a muffled cry, and then silence from the room.

"Karma's a bitch," said Jon quietly.

The men stared at the door. Even for seasoned combat veterans, it was maybe the most horrific thing they'd ever been a part of—they were all thankful they hadn't actually seen what was happening on the other side of the door.

Jon was kneeling next to Chris and looked over at him with wet cheeks. "My great grandparents died in Auschwitz. It's all I could think about when we were holding the doors closed," Jon whispered.

Chris nodded slightly. "Your great grandparents were murdered. What you just did saved 50,000 people—you remember that. Clear?"

"Yes, sir," he replied.

"Okay, people! On your feet! Ryan—you stand post and don't let anyone open those doors. The rest of you, on me!" Cascaes took off with his team close behind. There were still plenty of places to look.

With the upper deck secured, and most of the Qatari police and soldiers now assisting in detaining every vendor they saw until their box could be checked, the search on the lower deck went quickly. The dogs even hit on two boxes that had simply been abandoned by their would-be bombers who must have had too much time to think about their fate. By the time the game ended, there were Qatari security guards, cops, and soldiers at every confiscated box, moving the crowd through the tunnels and out of the stadium. Many of the fans were venting their anger at their horrible experience in the stadium. The jumbotrons hadn't worked since halfway through the first half; there had been no play-by-play announcing or any kind of audio; there was zero Wi-Fi or cell reception—it was outrageous! The tickets were expensive and while the game had been a thriller, the stadium was "garbage."

The team exited the stadium to their waiting Black Hawk, but left their two EODs on site with their K9 partners. As the men made their way to the Black Hawks, another bird touched down nearby, and four more EODs from Al Udeid hopped out to assist.

Cascaes told them where to find their comrades inside the stadium and hopped aboard his bird with the others. The Black Hawk rose up and made a beeline back to Al Udeid.

From above, Mackey and the others in the Prowler could see the birds heading in and out, as the stadium emptied out into the parking lots. At Mackey's request, the pilot asked for another crew to replace them and run electronic jamming so they could return to base. Twenty minutes later, they were joined by Moon Dog One, who took over their mission. Mackey and his crew were on the ground at Al Udeid only fifteen minutes behind the Black Hawk.

CHAPTER 49

Al Udeid

When the Black Hawk touched down, the base was still frantic with activity. Fire control teams in Hazmat suits had let the cars burn themselves out, and hopefully most of the poison gas with them. When the fires died down, they smothered the cars with foam and kept everyone back. Rescue personnel in protective gear had recovered the bodies of the two fallen Marine guards, who were taken to the hospital to be pronounced and prepared for their final trips home. Marine combat teams had been stationed around the perimeter, and Cobra gunships circled the desert looking for would-be attackers. The tension and anger showed in the faces of the Marines who had lost two brave brothers who refused to retreat from their post.

Cascaes and his men arrived back at their barracks to shower and change, and Mackey walked in behind them. They caught each other up quickly on the events at the stadium and the capture of Abdul Aziz. As soon as Mackey heard about Aziz being taken alive, he called Dex on his secure laptop so he could face to face chat with Dex and Kim. It took fifteen minutes for Cascaes to explain to them what had gone down at the stadium. Dex and Kim were amazed that none of the bombs had gone off.

"It's simply the greatest counter terrorism mission I've ever heard of," said Kim. "There would have been tens of thousands of casualties."

Mackey nodded. "And it would have been seen *live* all over the world."

Dex shrugged. "Actually, the Prowler knocked out the television transmission. Fans all over the world never got to see the game. I imagine there's a lot of pissed off football fans in Manchester and Madrid right about now."

"I won't lose sleep over it," said Kim. "We've been in touch with the Qataris. They're more than ecstatic with the success of your mission and the assistance of the US government."

"Great," said Cascaes dryly. "Maybe they'll lower the price of gas."

"Don't get crazy," said Dex sarcastically. "I have a bird in the air headed to pick up Abdul Aziz."

"Taking him to Gitmo?" asked Mackey.

Dex was stone faced. "Where *he's* going, Gitmo would be a vacation. We *will* find out whatever is inside his head. Which brings us to your next job."

Mackey scowled. "Whatcha got?"

"Right before your guys bagged Aziz, he made a phone call. We traced it. The number was outside Riyadh."

"We playing baseball?" asked Mackey.

"Negative. You'll be transported to Eskan and I'll brief you when you get there. This will be strictly a commando mission. We *have* the ring leader. What's left are strictly soldiers. These are enemy combatants and will be terminated. You'll go in before sunup, assault, and un-ass back to Eskan where you will be flown home. Is your team good to go?"

Mackey looked at Cascaes. They were all exhausted—drained emotionally, physically, and mentally; just another day at the office. "We have one minor wounded—just a scratch. We're good to go."

"Transport plane will be waiting for you at the airstrip in three hours. Eat, shower, pack, and get your asses to Eskan. We'll talk again in a few hours. Out."

The sun had set on Qatar, and the base was eerily quiet. A brief ceremony was held to honor the two fallen Marines. Patrols moved around the perimeter, but everyone knew that the attack was over.

The team headed back out to the airstrip where a Gulfstream C20 sat fueled and ready to go. To everyone's surprise, the base commander, Lieutenant General Houston, was there waiting for them as well. He snapped a salute at the team and shook hands with Mackey, pulling him close.

"Navy All-Stars, my ass. Thank you for what you did out here," he said quietly.

"Thank you, sir," replied Mackey, and with that, they loaded and took off for Eskan in Riyadh.

CHAPTER 50

The team landed at the airbase in Riyadh and bussed it to Eskan Village where they headed to their barracks. The men, although weary, made no mention of having had a long day. They changed into black tactical assault gear, Kevlar vets, and checked and loaded weapons. At oh-three hundred, they headed back to the airfield where two stealth Black Hawks were waiting for them.

Earl Jones was given the night off, to which he objected, but he still had a few stitches in his arm and was told to wait for their return. The rest of them piled into the two helicopters, as per their plan, and lifted off into the darkness heading northwest.

The call from Abdul Aziz had been made to a cell phone in an older part of Riyadh, somewhat on the outskirts of the city. It was a quasi-residential area that bordered on the desert. There were a few stores and commercial buildings mixed in, as well as two small mosques. Since tracing the call, Langley had listened to everything else that had gone in and out of that number, but it wasn't much. Most importantly, the phone hadn't moved from its original location. Apparently, the people on that end of the phone were sitting tight, waiting for Abdul Aziz to show up.

They'd have different guests.

The plan called for landing the birds in a small clearing, and the team crossing a small open area to the target house, which was inconveniently placed very close to its neighbors.

The small stone home was one story, and best analyst guesses concluded it couldn't house more than eight to ten adults. The team would enter the front and rear doors at the same time, confirm the location by calling the cell number once inside and listening for an answer, and once they were sure they were in the correct place, they would terminate all targets. The team hated missions like this—there was no honor in killing sleeping, defenseless human beings; but they tempered their emotions by remembering that the NWJ had planned on killing as many civilians as possible in the stadium, not to mention their brothers at Al Udeid.

The helicopters moved silently through the warm night air, flying only a couple of hundred feet above the desert floor to stay under radar, even though their Black Hawk was almost invisible to radar anyway, and touched down almost imperceptibly on the hard, sun baked ground. They hopped off and moved in total silence to the house. Cascaes and half the team moved around to the front of the house, keeping a watchful eye out for any civilians outside. Mackey and his crew moved to the rear door. Moose was on his knees at the door, checking his watch. In the next moment, he very slowly tried the door. It wasn't locked. A dim light was coming from down a center hallway. It was an oil lamp most likely as it came from the floor and not an overhead light.

Up in the front of the house, Cascaes looked at his watch. Jon was on his knee in front of Cascaes, his hand on the doorknob. Cascaes tapped Jon on his shoulder, who then tried the front door. It also opened, unlocked. Cascaes dialed the number of the cell phone he had been given. Inside, a tired voice mumbled something, which contained the word "Abdul" in it. They thought he was calling in.

A few more voices.

Another light came on, brighter.

Jon and Eric slipped inside the house and moved silently. Cascaes tapped his throat mic twice, signaling Mackey that the call was confirmed. After Cascaes signaled, everything happened quickly. Moose and Ripper moved through the rear door and stepped into a room on their right where three men had been sleeping on the floor, and were now getting up to greet Abdul Aziz. In the dim light, the red dots showed brightly on their foreheads. Moose and Ripper double-tapped each target, their silenced weapons making muffled pops in the quiet house.

Jon and Eric stepped into the front of the house and heard the pops. So did the men in the front room who began shouting to each other. Cascaes and Ernie P. rushed in and looked left as Jon and Eric moved right. One of the men had managed to get to his AK47 in the dark, but the second his hand touched it he was dead. The next thirty seconds were close-quarters killing all over the residence. Cascaes called "clear" in the smoky front of the house, followed by Mackey repeating it in the back of the house. The house smelled of cordite and blood.

The men moved quickly through the house, looking for anything that might be useful. They grabbed four cell phones and a laptop computer. They left the weapons, basic assault rifles that were common all over the Middle East, and scrambled back to the waiting Black Hawks. Dogs had started barking when the silenced weapons began popping off, and the team ran as fast as they could to the birds to get out of the neighborhood before any curious neighbors showed up. By the time the first light came on in the neighbor's house, the team was 300 feet off the desert and headed for their airbase.

The two Black Hawks landed back at the base at oh-four forty. The men hopped the same buses back to Eskan Village and were showered and snoring by 5:15. At 9, they were up and repacked, wearing Navy All-Star Baseball Team uniforms. They grabbed a quick breakfast and boarded a jet for home.

CHAPTER 51

Cascaes and Mackey sat with Kim and Dex back in Langley. The dark circles under their eyes were testament to their long flight after a grueling week. All four of them drank large cups of coffee.

Dex took a long sip, as he carefully chose his words. "Your team has proven itself in more ways than one. I have to admit, I was nervous about this whole concept—so many operators working in one place at one time. But the baseball cover was perfect, and your team's actions under pressure were truly outstanding. When you have time to write the full report, I'll spend a nice long weekend reading it. How you managed to prevent the stadium attack is beyond me."

"A little luck, a little help, and a whole lot of time training," said Cascaes.

"Well, it was amazing work. I have a special reward for you. The best movie you'll watch all year."

"Movie?" asked Mackey.

"Yes. Sorry I don't have popcorn. Kim will fill you in."

Kim leaned forward on her elbows and looked at both men thoughtfully. "Prince Abdul bin-Mustafa Awadi funded one hundred million dollars to the New Wahhabi Jihad. We all knew it, but we needed proof. The information we were able to pull from his computers, thanks to your bugging devices, gave us that proof. In addition, the laptop and cell phones you pulled from the safe house in Riyadh had lots of cell phone calls to the prince, as well as a network of New Wahhabi Jihadists and weapons dealers, including the now deceased Abu Mohamed. They were connected in multiple ways like a giant spider web. Lastly, Abdul Aziz had a few things to share."

"You got him to talk, huh?" asked Mackey. "Moose told me about wanting to kick his ass personally."

"The United States doesn't condone torture," said Kim, stone-faced.

"*Ohhh,* so you asked him nicely and he decided to share?" asked Cascaes.

"Medically enhanced interviews can divulge great amounts of information without inflicting any pain on the subject interviewee," said Kim, still keeping a poker face.

"I see. Any side effects of this technique?" asked Cascaes.

"Sometimes the subject may have permanent brain damage. It can be fatal," she replied coldly. They all stared at each other.

Dex interrupted the awkward silence. "Abdul Aziz confirmed that the prince was giving him the money. It was the icing on the cake to prove our case."

"Prove it to whom?" asked Mackey.

"Prove it to the people above our pay grade that make certain decisions," replied Dex. "Kim, finish, please."

"As you know, Prince Awadi loves his very expensive racing cars," said Kim.

The two men nodded, perplexed, and waited until she continued.

"We let it leak that the new Zenvo 10 was available in Riyadh."

"What's a Zenvo 10?" asked Mackey.

Kim smiled. "It's your basic one and a half million dollar Danish racing car. It's so fast it needs computerized steering and braking assistance. You're basically sitting in a rocket car, and at 250 miles an hour, most drivers can't operate the car without the car automatically helping out the driver."

"Okay, so where's this going?" asked Mackey.

"As soon as the prince heard it was in Saudi Arabia, he had to have it immediately. The dealership failed to mention that our toy department had the vehicle for a few weeks first."

The two men sat back and folded their arms almost simultaneously.

"*Okay*...?" said Mackey, waiting for the rest of the story.

Kim picked up a remote and pressed the run button. A stunning white sports car was racing through the wide open desert highway. She turned up the sound, and loud American music was playing.

"This was recorded yesterday. The prince likes to listen to Led Zeppelin when no one is around. Just another one of his little secrets."

"The car is bugged?" asked Cascaes.

"Yup," said Kim, with an evil smile.

They watched for another minute, listening to loud music and the prince's terrible singing.

"He's doing almost 250 miles an hour at this point," said Kim.

"How can you tell? The speedometer monitored, too?" asked Cascaes.

"Nope. But the Moon Dogs flying overhead can tell his exact speed."

Mackey's eyes lit up. "You said computer-assisted steering, didn't you?"

"Why *yes*, yes I did," she said, her smile now a full-fledged grin. She pressed another button. The audio added another layer of sound over the prince's terrible singing.

"Lima one, this is Moon Dog Five. We're in position with target confirmed."

"Moon Dog Five, you are cleared to begin electronic jamming," said a female voice. It was Kim Elton's voice. She smiled at the two Chrises.

"Moon Dog Five, commencing attack, over."

There was a few seconds of chatter in the cockpit, followed by screaming from the inside of the car as the driver realized he was no longer in charge of his vehicle. The aerial footage showed the white car veering off the highway, never slowing down as it put up a huge cloud of dust and sand behind it. The car continued across the flat expanse of desert straight for a small cliff that dropped to a rocky bottom. The prince's screaming drowned out the Led Zeppelin classic "When the Levee Breaks."

The beautiful white sports car exploded into a giant fireball when it hit the rocks at almost 250 miles an hour.

"Not sure if airbags or a seatbelt will help," said Kim calmly. "He wanted to kill 50,000 civilians. I'm going to go home, take a nice warm bath, and sleep about ten hours. I think you and your guys should take a few days off, too. You deserve it."

Chris and Mackey stared at the last freeze-framed picture of the burning wreckage.

"So the folks above your pay grade wanted the prince gone, but wanted it to look like an accident," said Cascaes, basically talking to himself.

"Allegedly," said Dex.

"So that's everyone except the Qatari Emir," added Mackey. He started counting off on his fingers, "Abu Mohamed the arms dealer, Prince Awadi the money guy, Abdul Aziz the killer, most of the New Wahhabi Jihad, the Sarin—it's done?"

Dex sat back and folded his fingers together. "The Qatari Emir will be rethinking his connections with the radicals, I'm sure. The stadium attack would have crippled any chances for a World Cup or tourist business, and the fact that his buddy the prince 'had an accident' won't be lost on him, either. I think the emir has seen the light. It was a very successful mission, gentlemen." Dex took a moment to find the rights words, and then he smiled. "Mr. Hill has been reassigned by Director Holstrum. Seems there had been some differences of opinion that didn't go Mr. Hill's way."

"You must be heartbroken," said Mackey. "You forgot one additional victory. We beat the prince's team on the baseball field," said Mackey.

"With corked bats," reminded Cascaes.

"They had ringers!" Mackey exclaimed.

Chris shrugged. "I'm sure we'll get a chance to play again."

"Maybe," said Dex. "But not any time soon. Your team is headed to South America in a few weeks. And you won't be a baseball team."

"A new cover story?" asked Mackey.

"Missionaries," replied Dex with a smile.

The two Chrises looked at each other.

"Lord help us," was all Mackey could muster.